WITH LOVE, LEO

MILO LORIEN

Milo Lorien, LLC
A VOICE FROM INSIDE

With Love, Leo

DEDICATION

This novel is dedicated to her. It is my sincerest hope that in some way, through this novel, I can be there for her when I unintentionally bring her the ultimate pain and heartbreak. There is no way to avoid it.

Noodle, may you find a way to begin your next chapter when the one you shared with me is concluded. I will always love and adore you,
Eternally Yours,
Leo.

WHO IS MILO LORIEN?

Milo Lorien is a neurodiverse author of Latino heritage. He is a husband, father, and disabled Marine.

His American dream was sidelined by military service-related injuries in his early 30's, including PTSD, TBI, Neurocognitive Disorder, chronic nerve/muscle pain, and constant tremors. He would be forced to give up on a career. Milo's condition worsens daily as his memory loss and an overall deficit in his ability to communicate effectively declines.

With the support of his loving wife, he writes in the hopes of capturing his love, his suffering, and his hope so the world can learn from his struggles before social isolation leaves his journey forgotten.

PROLOGUE

I will never forget the moment I heard, "Excuse me, do you have the time?" When I looked up, I was enchanted. There I was, staring into the face of the most beautiful human being I had yet to encounter. She barely noticed me, but ever the consummate gentleman, I provided the time. I could not believe the heartache I felt as I watched her walk away. I didn't know her name or anything about her. What I did know is that I could spend the rest of my life listening to the song of her voice and most definitely watching her walk, but alas, she was gone.

I didn't know it then, but the universe had a different plan for us. It would bring us together, and I did not pass up a chance to get to know her. In short order, we fell in love, and after several attempts to propose, she would eventually say yes.

In my heart, I had planned on giving her the world. I would work endlessly to give her the life she deserved, but she would become my caregiver in the end.

For my part, instead of giving her the world, I would inundate her with a litany of needs and medical diagnoses that would require never-ending sacrifices of her. I would never live up to all my romantic promises, and yet, she would never leave my side.

CHAPTER
ONE

A NEW DAWN

It's Saturday morning. The Blue Hour has arrived, and Julia is sitting in silence at the small round table. A few vacant chairs sit around the table, and the large windows surrounding her allow Julia to overlook the yard.

With a glance at her husband's empty seat, she remembers the way Leo used to smile at her across the table. Together, they'd discuss their plans for the day while enjoying their coffee. Her husband would comment on the weather outside, and then he'd turn his attention to predicting what the morning news cycle would bring. Julia always enjoyed hearing his thoughts on the issues of the day. Leo had a way with words that reminded her of his unfilled potential.

Small streams of sunlight begin to stake their claim to the darkness, Leo's favorite time of day.

He'd often say, "People have this fascination with the sunset that I'll never understand. If I could manage to keep a schedule, I would be up to watch the Blue Hour every day."

While it was difficult for Leo to keep a schedule, he did try.

Julia would always reply, "Why is that, dear?"

She knew the answer, but he always seemed a bit energized when he answered. She very much enjoyed that side of him.

Such excitement and passion had grown rare as his condition worsened. To counter, Julia had taken to making mental notes of what conversations affected him so. Through some experimentation, she learned the most effective questions to ask and when.

It might seem a bit manipulative, but as his wife, one love, and best friend, she knew he didn't mind. It was he who gave her the idea. Early on, he had mentioned things he liked and ways she might use it to her advantage down the road.

How right he was.

"It's quite simple," he'd say. "Sundown, or the Golden Hour, is the end of the day. It's beautiful, to be sure. One should take every opportunity to greet the end of the day with thanks when given a chance. Strong, proud, with a feeling of accomplishment. Regardless of the scale of accomplishment, one should celebrate. Take stock at every opportunity of whatever it might be that you've accomplished. Never forget that even the smallest phone call is an accomplishment. One that would otherwise remain for tomorrow."

He continued, "Yet, the beginning of the day brings with it the Blue Hour. Greeting the sun on the horizon as it begins its daily journey—a meeting to refresh one's photon energy reserves. A new day, a new breath, and a blessing from the warm sun. That is how I'd want to greet every morning."

"SAYING GOODBYE IS IMPORTANT. With it, goes lost opportunities and a farewell to that which may never be again. Yet, saying hello brings with it new opportunities and hope for what the future may hold. The possibilities are back on the table each morning. So every morning, one should ask themselves. What will I do before the sun sets once again."

Letting him ramble on about the possibilities for his future was one of the few meaningful gifts Julia could bestow.

He would often end with, "I know I'll never do these things, but it's nice to think about."

Fading as it begins, the Blue Hour sets the stage. As the sunlight crawls its way like a dimmer switch, the light grows in both intensity and coverage.

Until finally, it fills the kitchen with reenergizing light and warmth. Despite the shining sun and singing birds, the shadow of his absence hangs heavy in the room.

Amid such wondrous memories, Julia is frozen in amber, unable to do anything at all. She thought she would have gotten used to it after he moved to The Mountain, the assisted living home. At least there, she was able to join him, but now, it has been several weeks since Leo left The Mountain on his journey past the rim.

That is where Leo believed he would go next. His take on dying. His final journey across the frontier of all knowledge. Into a place where everything is unknown. He often referred to his death as his "Journey Beyond The Rim" and promised that he would reach out if he were able.

JULIA DOESN'T FEEL like doing the things they usually did. Watching their morning shows or having coffee all seems futile. She doesn't know what to do with herself now that he is gone.

This is the part of their morning where they would meet and greet the day. Leo had not been gone that long. Though now that he is gone, she isn't sure how to proceed. For so long, he was her partner in life. They shared everything--hopes, dreams, successes, failures--*everything*.

That is until he began the transformation from partner to charge.

When the change happened, she was almost a mother to him. He, in turn, became a child. The age of his behavior was dependent on the day, his locations, and even those in his proximity. The variation of these 'personas' was prone to change from one to another on a whim.

So much time and effort over many years.

What will she do now?

THE DOORBELL RINGS and their dog begins barking.

It takes Julia a minute to determine, in her head, who is at the door. She can't think of anyone she feels is worth her getting up. They usually go away if she ignores it.

Not today.

Today it's her friend, Donna Martin. Donna lets herself in so Julia doesn't have to move. Not that she would have anyway.

"Julia, honey, where are you?"

Julia doesn't answer because she doesn't feel like talking to anyone, even Donna.

Donna is her best friend. Julia not answering won't stop her from continuing further. Julia can hear Donna, but it all sounds like noise.

Wait, what day is it? Julia wonders.

Julia barely even noticed the passage of time this morning. Donna must be stopping by on her way to work.

Julia and Donna, while best friends, rarely talk to each other day in and day out. Their contact is infrequent at most. They are like a secure, married couple whose lives are separate. Sometimes their friendship is bicoastal, and other times, it's across town. The one thing they never do is pretend, though.

LEO HAD FOUND it strange they didn't intertwine their lives like he imagined best friends do. In truth, he'd never had a best friend aside from Julia. There were some from his youth, but they weren't the kind of best friend you hung out with for a long time. A friendship that doesn't change despite each person evolving and living life. The type of friend with whom little changes in the absence of recent communication.

Having moved more than most throughout his youth, he missed out on that kind of friendship. Though he did have many close friends growing up, his moving around cost him a certain longevity.

He grew up at a time when maintaining contact long-distance was costly. The choices were either letter writing or expensive telephone calls. Neither he nor his friends were able to afford telephone bills. Most were not skilled letter writers.

"Nowadays, people take for granted the ease at which you can reach out to one another--let alone visit," he'd say.

He would often tease Julia. "Donna must have been a friend from before you entered Witness Protection." He often said they were trying to keep their friendship from the world.

Julia would say, "We talk when we need to and visit when we have time. What's wrong with that?"

Leo never had a comeback because there wasn't anything wrong with it. They have been good friends for many years.

Whatever their friendship was, it worked for them. Leo never saw any drama between them, and they always sought each other out in difficult times.

All the while, they maintained their own lives, and their friendship never took a hit. Leo was often a little jealous of Donna. Not of their friendship exactly. Instead, it was the seamless shorthand and connection Julia had with Donna.

He'd sometimes joke in that self-deprecating way that he was nothing more than a stand-in for Donna. She felt it was one more thing his illness took from him--his pride and confidence.

For some reason she could never quite put her finger on, Leo had been terrified that if he weren't careful, she would find someone better and leave him. Sure, they'd had ups and downs over the years, but nothing she thought should warrant those feelings. Julia believed the real source of those fears were hidden away in his past well before she'd met him.

Leo would make self-deprecating jokes when he was feeling this way. Often, they would end in a not-so-subtle reminder of their marriage contract.

Leo always responded the same way, "Too late. The contract says forever."

To which, Julia would respond, "Whatever helps you sleep, darling."

She'd then tell him, "Don't be a dufus." Then, changing the conversation, she'd grab the paper's sales flyers. With a devilish grin, Julia would say, "Honey, look, those 3D printers you wanted are on sale. Should we get one? Donna said they are miracle workers."

Leo would laugh. "You are one funny lady." He'd then faux storm off with a smile and say, "I know I'm your man."

It was all in jest as she'd remind him. "Only you can do what you do for me, baby." Julia knew it was juvenile and shallow, but the male ego is fragile.

Julia never overlooked that even in the most confident of men, a small comment can go a long way towards good or bad. The 25 years they'd spent together taught Julia how to navigate his ego.

Still, some days it was almost like handling Phyllo dough. Delicate and ruined with little effort.

This little dance was not helped by Donna. Always taunting Leo that she "would steal Julia away one day if he wasn't careful."

Donna had no romantic interest in Julia. It was more about stealing Julia to go on a cruise or see a male dance show. That was the threat.

Julia knew it was Donna's way of stirring up trouble. Not real trouble. Rather, the kind only considered entertaining to good friends.

Donna and Leo had a friendship built on their stereotypical interactions. Sitting here now, watching Donna around the house, Julia missed the play fights.

. . .

DONNA'S MOVING ABOUT as she does. Full of life and happiness.

How vile? Julia thinks. *How can anyone have that kind of energy?*

Walking around, picking things up, and making coffee, she babbles on about the day. She also comments on the guests from Leo's gathering. Donna goes on about people and happenings. She could come across as shallow and gossipy sometimes. Her problem is that she cares about people, and that leads to her getting overly involved.

Julia knows deep down that Donna doesn't mean anything by it. Yet, at the moment, she finds her best friend annoying.

Why can't that shrew take her happy feelings somewhere else? She just wants to be alone.

No. What Julia wants is to be sitting here with Leo, but that is not to be.

AT THAT MOMENT, Donna sits down with two coffees. She places one in front of Julia and gives her friend a big hug. For a fleeting moment, there seems to be normalcy. Instantly, it's like past mornings when she'd stop by after Leo left for work.

Julia is disappointed that a cup of coffee and a hug from her best friend can remind her. A small glimpse of her ordinary world amid the shattered glass of her life.

She looks at her smiling friend, who says, "There you are, honey."

All she can get out is, "What do I do now?"

The only thing Julia wants to do is talk about him, think about him, and speak to Leo. She doesn't know what to make of his life ending far too soon, the advanced warning notwithstanding.

Donna's reply is simple and yet profound. "Just breathe." Donna suddenly stands. "That reminds me," Donna says. "I'll be right back."

Donna now has her attention.

She watches as her best friend walks into their den and pulls out a small box from the closet. Stepping back, Donna has a smile on her face that Julia doesn't understand.

When Donna sits back down, she begins to regale Julia with a story.

"I know you probably don't want to hear this right now, but I promised," Donna says.

"What are you talking about?" Julia asks her, perplexed.

Donna says, "That hubby of yours. We may not have always agreed, and I might have hassled him a time or two, but he was special. He loved you in a way that made me a little jealous every time I came over here. Even when Leo annoyed me, I never realized how genuine his love for you was. Any time he had hurt you, I'd be the first to call for his beheading. Honestly, after spending the afternoon with him, I know two things for certain. His love for you was as genuine as I am likely ever to witness."

"And the second thing?" Julia asks.

"Oh right," Donna continues, "that one is easy. I forgave him for all his past transgression and any he might have made after our chat."

Julia is stunned. She says, "Well, you two must have had some afternoon. Care to explain why I shouldn't take off these earrings right now?" With a stern 'Let's have it' look, she just stares at Donna.

Julia is clearly being humorous, and all Donna can do is burst into laughter.

With her hand on her belly, Donna's laughter grows infectious. All a part of Donna's treacherous plan.

Donna seized on an opportunity to get Julia to smile and laugh? It wasn't intentional on Donna's part, but she couldn't pass up an opportunity that presented itself.

Julia can't resist and begins to laugh. Hard and constant.

The idea of Donna with Leo was certainly laughable. Preposterous really, but in that split second, Julia doesn't even seem to notice. For one small moment, she isn't sad over Leo's departure but rather embroiled in a moment with her friend.

Catching her breath, Donna reaches for some tissues. Handing Julia a few, she says, "First off, you aren't wearing earrings. But trust me when I tell you--this new look you're sporting is scary enough." Julia doesn't find it funny and tosses the tissues at her friend.

"Until this promise," Donna continues, "I used to worry about the amount of attention he showed you. I feared it was too much. I was concerned it was a sign of something troubling.

He was always calling you 'My Love' or answering you with 'How can I be of service today?' I mean, who does that? Truthfully, I didn't think guys like Leo were real. I felt a need to doubt him because I'd never met anyone like him."

Donna continues, "For that, I apologized to him, or at least I tried. He explained more about his condition. After that, I realized that the man I didn't like was ruled by the 'faulty vehicle--his Chango.' I told him I forgave anything he thought he needed my forgiveness for. I never accurately fathomed what you both had to go through. Leo had his 'split personalities' but you--having to hold onto your true love in a sea of personalities and memories...."

"Now, as for the talk of forgiveness, Leo wouldn't even entertain the discussion," Donna says. "He told me that 'A lady should never apologize for being cautious or deferring to her intuition. Women have plenty of reasons to do just that. The burden of earning your trust on an individual basis resides with us. Hopefully, the example we set now will lessen the burdens on future generations of both genders. After all, in the final analysis--how we behave now will have a long and lasting impact on humankind's progeny.'"

"Always saying weird stuff, that Leo of yours," Donna says.

"You shut up," Julia replies.

Donna pauses for a minute to clean up. Julia and Donna's eyes both have tears in them. Reaching across the table, Julia grabs her hand.

Donna looks over at Julia and says, "I forgot just how much Leo could surprise you when he got deep."

Her husband was certainly prone to going to some deep and heavy places in his thoughts. Julia always found his mind to be his sexiest attribute. Even when it began failing him, Leo still had his moments.

Leo would say, "The closer I get to the Rim, the more sense everything makes."

GRAND GESTURES

In the years since Leo became ill, Julia had enjoyed telling others about her husband. She wanted everyone to know who he was and who he could have been.

She also took every opportunity to explain to anyone who would ask.

As far as Julia is concerned, who her Leo had become and why he did the things he did were every bit as important as where he grew up and what he used to do for work. The good and bad were mashed up to create her Leo. It was not only the things he did, both good and bad, but how he handled them. These are valuable lessons for others.

It might seem strange, but Leo believed the purpose in life was simple. Consider, Create, Contribute; his mission statement.

He'd argue the most effective way to combat it was to start simple.

"Consider the problems of the world around you," he'd say.

Leo would suggest that starting nearby gave a particular motivation to someone's creative process. The problems should be something that impacts someone personally. If they find no pressing need, then they move to their neighbors and their neighbor's neighbors.

He'd urge people to ask themselves, "What problems are closest to you that could benefit from your particular skills?"

Leo reasoned that once someone found a problem in their wheelhouse, they stood a better chance of contributing or creating a solution. He would caution that this is not a binary approach and requires flexibility.

View the problem via a perspective of their strengths and weaknesses. "How can you aid in solving this problem?" Leo would ask.

The final step is just as simplistic.

When someone knows what problem they want to address, it's easy to jump online and find non-profit organizations where their help may be useful. Once they contact the organizations and find they are a good fit, they can then help solve the problem.

Toward the end, Leo would say, "Can you imagine if all these tweets and things were focused on solving the world's problems? Crowdsource, I think they call it. I would name it, 'A Table in Alexandria.' You might not like it, but it reminds me of what might've happened had that vast library not burned."

Julia didn't want people to remember him in his worst stages, but she never shied away from a conversation about him. People are ignorant of those like him, and she'd be damned if she is going to enable them. Of course, any real conversation is impossible with some people, but thankfully, those aren't as predominant.

In most cases, people pretended to care and be empathetic, but mostly they didn't believe Leo was all that bad. They treated him as though he was malingering because they could not grasp a man his age having his kind of problems.

Visually, he appeared well aside from his military injury, which had left him using a cane. There were times when his physical movements made his pain levels visible. Though his mental deterioration wasn't always apparent, and anyone who spent less than 10-20 minutes at a time with him might never have noticed it.

'Invisible disabilities,' they call it now.

Julia was always thankful to have found a husband whom she desired for his mind. She'd learned in her youth the invaluable lesson of putting too much 'weight' on the physical alone - No pun intended.

Unfortunately, there were many unintended consequences. In their case, Julia and Leo faced having the marital bed dismantled as Leo's brain got worse. Over time, she realized that while Leo was still a handsome man, what he now lacked were the qualities Julia found most alluring. All the logic in the world couldn't give one the subtle 'feel goods' that bring a couple together in that way.

Illnesses like these change a person enough to make the people around them see a slightly different person in the body of a loved one. This makes it difficult for most to interact with a loved one in such intimate ways.

Julia often thinks about the man she fell in love with versus who everyone believed him to be.

Leonard Sebastian Runkel was the love of her life. 'Love of her life' is maybe stretching it, but Julia and Leo were about being real. As best they could, they had always tried to remember that. It may not always go the way they'd hoped, but together they never gave up.

Julia couldn't say Leo was 'the one who got away.' That slot had long been filled in her life, but that was one thing about Leo. As much as he wanted to be that guy, he never made Julia feel like she had to pretend he was.

One more reason she loved him immensely. Leo always knew that while he and Julia fit perfectly, a part of Julia's heart would never be his. He knew her fantasies and dreams did not always have a role for him.

Leo also knew that Julia had proved to be the one person who always had his back. Without a doubt, they were best friends. Like two leaves independently reaching for the sun to nourish their souls, his wife would never reach so far as to detach from the shared branch. The journey they vowed to take together was the same path they traveled to the very end. Julia would have had it no other way.

Leo was not what one would consider a manly man. He was a good-looking guy. Not the kind women fawn over, but certainly enjoyable to look at. He had no interest in sports, and while he was not a social butterfly, everyone liked him. Julia admired that about him. He was his own man and required no validation from anyone, aside from Julia.

IN THE BEGINNING, it was normal, but as he declined, it became his blanket. The sound of her words alone put Leo's mind and soul at ease for what ailed him. She was his beacon.

When Julia first met Leo, he didn't speak all that much. Later, she learned that Leo wasn't much for small talk. He conversed wonderfully--asked questions, and genuinely wanted to get to know her. He didn't engage in gossip, and he had beautifully deep thoughts about love and life. Julia found him wise well beyond his young years. Years which gave her plenty of pause on their own. Yet his wisdom and words would eventually help win her heart.

Leo's behaviors would seal the deal, though. Early in their relationship, he would open her car door and carry her books. Anything, just anything to be around her.

As their relationship progressed, he would do things she never dreamed of in a relationship.

Leo would sit near her bathtub and talk to her. For as long as she wanted. Sometimes she just wanted him to listen, and he would offer no feedback of consequence.

When she was ready to get out, he would leave and return

with bottles of water. Julia liked to drink cold water after a hot bath.

On select occasions after Julia finished her post-bath shower, she would dry off and meet Leo in the bedroom.

Leo would settle upon the bed and get comfortable up against the headboard. When Julia was ready, she would snuggle up between his legs in the middle of the bed.

Sitting there in between Leo's legs, after finding the perfect movie, Leo would spin her around and whip it out--Julia's favorite hairbrush. They would cozy up and watch the movie while Leo brushed out her hair. It, too, would fade over time, but those were some of Julia's happiest intimate moments with her Leo.

Got away this one did not.

LEO WANTED to learn more about everyone and everything but had no desire to be in the spotlight. He always wanted to help yet preferred to leave the credit to others. Leo enjoyed helping; he just didn't want everyone to know about it.

Julia was never quite sure what to make of him. Being around him always felt natural, and he always kept things interesting.

A few years after they were married, Leo took out a large ad in the local newspaper. When Julia saw the credit card charge, she asked him about it.

"Leo, honey, did you buy an ad in the newspaper? I mean, I know you did--I see it, but what's it for?"

Leo replied, "Yes, my dear, I did. Unfortunately, I can't tell you about it just yet. I hope you understand and trust me. Give me a few days." Leo kissed her, hugged her, and said, "Is that ok?"

Julia knew that he wasn't trying to hide the charge, so she said, "Of course I trust you, but now I'm curious. I look forward to it."

He smiled and went back to his office.

A few days later, it was Valentine's Day, and Julia had forgotten. She had a bad habit of getting lost in her work, and Leo was ok with that.

Though in this instance, Julia had forgotten to get him anything. It was lunchtime, so she figured she'd step out of the office and pick him something up.

When Julia got back to her office, Janice, her colleague, said, "Hey girl, what did you do for lunch?" She explained the whole gift situation, and Janice said, "I hope it's awesome."

"Of course it is; his loving wife bought it for him." She smiled and showed her.

Janice replied, "Oh, that's nice."

The gift was a small figurine from one of his favorite sci-fi shows. Leo liked to collect the starships and characters from his shows, and this one he'd not been able to find.

It was perfect.

Little did they know then that such trinkets would help keep him bound to his life.

All the ladies in Julia's office knew of Leo. His random flower deliveries and surprise visits were legendary.

Leo lacked certain boundaries when it came to sending her flowers for no apparent reason. It tended to cause a stir among the ladies and their husbands who were informed of his actions after.

The other husbands often joked about putting a hit out on him '… if he doesn't quit making us look bad.'

A few minutes later, Janice returned, handing her a newspaper.

Julia had forgotten all about that advertisement Leo bought. She braced herself.

She had caught the eyes of a few ladies who had cheeky smirks on their faces.

"Oh my god, he didn't!" Julia shouted. Giggles could be heard all around her.

One lady yelled out, "You better be putting out tonight, or I'll have to stop by and do it for you." It was all in jest, and the ladies all laughed.

Julia shot her a look and half-heartedly waved her fist.

There, on the page of their local newspaper--not the front page but certainly where everyone would see it--Leo had published a full Valentine's Day love letter.

Julia now understood Leo's advertisement purchase.

He wanted the world to know of his love for Julia. He loved the grand gesture.

Sometimes it embarrassed her, and she didn't always like it, but Julia did love that he wanted to. She was flattered that he wanted everyone to know of his love for her. She just wouldn't tell him that.

She'd say, "He does not need any more encouragement."

Leo needed no additional encouragement to be a hopeless romantic. It was a side of him that had to grow on her.

She just looked over at Janice and mouthed the words, "Don't hate," with a big smile. Janice was unlikely to see these kinds of gestures from her husband, Jeff.

Rest assured, Julia and Leo had 'discussed' it when she got home, and he promised never to do it again--or else.

A voice brings Julia back to reality.

"Julia, what are you smiling at?" Donna asks in a loud voice while checking her phone.

"Nothing, Donna, please continue," she says.

"Julia, you are a liar, but I love you," Donna says, smiling at Julia.

It is a blessing and a curse to be unable to lie to a best friend. Leo called it the universe in balance.

"Okay, so," Julia continues, "Donna, are you going to tell me about this promise already?"

Putting her phone down on the table, Donna says, "So out of nowhere, one day, I got a phone call. It was from your grand-daughter, Nova."

Julia chimes in, "Oh, you don't say. So, she's been in on this the whole time, has she?" Julia's eyebrows raise in anticipation.

Donna continues, "Yes, she was. I gathered she was helping Leo while spending extra time with him through her work at The Mountain.

"Anyway, she told me that Leo would like to meet for a private lunch and asked that I tell no one, including you. Nova promised everything was fine and said Leo was planning a surprise for you and 'required my assistance.' Poor thing, she is so like her grandfather."

Donna and Julia giggle, and Julia's head movements confirm she concurs with that assessment.

"I showed up on the day in question. I think you were at work," she continues, "So he was saying all this stuff and telling me about what you've done for his life and how he loves you. Bear in mind, this was just after he'd moved into Elysian Fields Mountain, so that news had already put a damper on the tone of the conversation. At least for me. He didn't seem all that outwardly bothered by it. Then he looked at me, grabbed my hands, and said, 'Promise me you will be there for her when I am not.'"

Julia begins to tear up.

"Not yet just wait," Donna says, handing her a tissue.

THE MOUNTAIN

L eo had the strangest sensation.

Coming around, he was unsure of how long he'd been asleep.

As Leo's eyes were opening, he swore he could see someone walk to a small table that was set up in the corner. It was nothing elaborate—just a round table with four padded chairs.

Leo couldn't help but notice the chairs. They looked comfortable enough.

A man had set down a tray and left. For that split second, he wondered if his eyes were betraying him.

Leo couldn't argue the logic at work here. Who comes into a person's living room and leaves a tray of food? He looked around, wondering about this man in uniform.

Admittedly, it was a bit of a blur, but Leo was sure. He had seen some type of uniform and was equally confident it was a man. Or was it?

A woman in uniform? he thought.

The number of professions requiring a uniform informed his options.

Wait, he thought, *given the parameters, it could be a hospital.*

Looking around, Leo thinks, *Nope, this is not a hospital room.*

It was almost as though this person did not see Leo. Though, it was possible Leo was seen but ignored.

Leo continued to look around before he got up. He was on a couch, surrounded by furniture from his den. It looked like his den, at least, but something was off. He couldn't quite put his finger on it.

The television was showing one of his favorite science fiction shows.

Ah, there is the remote.

Leo hit the pause button and got up to see what was on the table.

As Leo approached the table, he noticed a breakfast bar in the kitchen. The other end of the kitchen connected to a simple hallway with a side table. The kind you might find in a foyer. It had a mirror above it, and on the surface was a small lamp and key dish. Leo found that odd since he hadn't carried keys in many years. The other end of the hallway looked like one bathroom across from two bedrooms.

This doesn't feel familiar.

At the table, he looked down to see a large round tray with plates of food. One plate had a large order of french fries, and the other had a hamburger precisely the way he liked it.

No pink inside with a great sear. Lettuce, bacon, and the sesame seed bun toasted with butter. It looked delicious, but one bite told Leo this was not made by his beautiful wife's hand. Yet he was hungry enough to eat it.

Eat it, he did.

Leo had not realized how hungry he was. It turns out the hamburger was not half bad. Leo could definitely eat this again.

He was still unsure of why he had room service. More importantly, what should he do with the plates? He was growing frustrated with the lack of information available to him. Leo put the dishes in the sink and figured he'd worry about it later.

He should see what's on television. Leo made his way back over to the sofa and sat down.

A few minutes later, there was a knock at the door. As he started getting up, Leo remembered he was watching television, so he hit play.

Oh, wait. There's another knock at the door, reminding him why he was getting up.

Answering the door, he met a cheerful young woman. Leo thought she seemed familiar somehow but wasn't sure how. She introduced herself as 'Nova' and asked if she could take his tray.

It's strange, right? he thought. *Why is a person coming and taking my tray away after I eat?*

Leo was caught between unsure and intuition, telling him to slam the door and run away. He was not very good in new situations. 'Change' was his mortal enemy. His alter ego 'Chango' thrived on the confusion brought on with 'change.' He liked to think of 'change' as his ultimate weakness.

Despite being unsure, he said, "Okay."

Leo didn't recognize any of the dishes, so they couldn't have been his. He told her he had put them in the sink, and Nova asked again, "Would it be okay if I came in and retrieved them, Mr. Runkel?"

Okay, stop. Exactly where am I?

As he looked around, he didn't recognize the place. All the things in it appeared to be his own, but it wasn't. And now, there was this young woman calling him by name.

He recalled an instance where he found himself in a similar situation. In that case, it was a hotel room, and he awoke to forget how he'd gotten there. He did not even realize it was a hotel room.

Leo remembered waking up in unfamiliar surroundings, and Julia was not there. A few moments later, Julia had come out of the bathroom after hearing Leo walking around. She knew this might happen in advance. Her experience had led to her planning for this type of event.

This memory left Leo compelled to ask.

"Excuse me, Nova," he said. "Would you be so kind as to explain why that man was bringing me food, and why are you now cleaning up after me?"

He noticed her uniform was different from the other guy's. It was business casual, like a front desk hotel clerk--very business casual. The blazer she wore had her name embroidered on the front right pocket. It read, 'Nova R.'

Leo noticed that Nova was taking the dishes out of the sink and placed them back on the tray. She continued tidying up everything else around her. When she'd finished, there was no trace of the food in the sink or on the counter. It was as if no one had used the space. Julia would love her cleaning skills.

Nova replied, "It is all part of the service here at Elysian Fields Mountain, or as we like to call it, 'The Mountain.'"

Leo had a confused look on his face.

Nova followed up with, "I know you only recently moved in, but I hope you like it here very much. Here is one of the brochures to reacquaint yourself in case you didn't get one." Then she moved toward the door.

Before leaving, Nova turned to Leo and said, "Mr. Runkel, would you mind if I hugged you. I'm a hugger, something I got from my grandpa. I called him 'Pop.' So that you know, you are my favorite tenant."

Leo instinctively replied, "Sure, sweetie." Opening his arms to offer a hug, he thought, *what am I doing? I don't know this young woman. What if someone misinterprets the hug?'* Yet, something about her felt familiar.

As she came in for a hug, Leo smiled. Nova smiled right back, but he could have sworn she had tears in her eyes. Strange. He hoped she was okay. Leo presumed she had a kind heart and was sad for the 'old man' in front of her. Emotions often come hand and hand with compassionate hearts. No doubt, her job called for both.

After a tight squeeze and a peck on the cheek, Nova turned and left.

WELL, what now? he thought, then it occurred to him--*Where is Julia?* His beautiful wife was nowhere to be seen.

The startling revelation induced a slight panic attack in Leo. Julia was his rock and tether to reality. He immediately went looking for his phone.

He found it on the dresser and could not help but notice the decor. On its surface, everything looked like home, but it was not the home he remembered.

In preparing to call his guardian angel, he made his way to the couch. After sitting, he took a sip of his coffee that he'd forgotten was there. It was a delicious instant cappuccino that Julia had always bought him. Delicious and easy to make. Though, now it was closer to cold than he preferred.

Leo noticed the brochure on the coffee table. Remembering Nova gave it to him, he flipped through it.

It looked as one might expect. Lots of pictures and a small 'Welcome to Elysian Fields Mountain' introduction. There were lists of services and facilities available to residents. As he read more, Leo realized that this was a ranch. A compound of sorts. It was made exclusively for people with neurological conditions, which leave them dependent on others.

Their mission is to provide the fullest measure of independence and privacy for residents and loved ones.

Hang on, where is Julia? Oh, right, I was going to call her. He grabbed his phone and hit his speed dial; it began ringing.

Wrapped in the warmest, most inviting voice, Julia said, "I see you," to which he replied, "I see you too." It was a greeting they'd adopted from a favorite film.

"Baby, where are you?" he said.

She replied, "Take a deep breath, tell me what is happening, and don't worry. Everything is just fine."

Leo had no real idea where it was coming from, but her words were enough, and his worry began to subside. Leo trusted Julia more than himself. He was not sure why he knew it had always been that way and that she'd never let him down before.

Leo assumed it was a gut feeling. He began to calm and focus on her words.

Julia said, "Do you happen to remember the problems you were having with your memory?"

He did.

Initially, Leo remembered that he had not worked for a very long time because of his back problems. Sometime later, he and Julia noticed other changes and put things together.

Thus, leading to the discovery that Leo had a neurological condition. It was a condition that would impact his behavior, his speech, his memory--everything.

He told Julia so, and she replied, "Well if you remember, we came up with a plan of what to do when I was unable to care for you around the clock any longer? That plan turned out to be 'The Mountain.'"

Her words hit Leo like a ton of bricks.

It may sound cliche, but it was fitting. Leo could remember thinking he had to figure out a way to prepare for getting worse. It was difficult to forget the burden he'd already been to his family. He imagined he would do whatever was necessary to alleviate that burden.

He informed Julia that he remembered pieces, and she replied, "You should go over the brochure Nova brought, so you can get better acquainted."

Julia continued, "I am only 15 minutes away from The Mountain, and Nova will come to visit every day. I will stay the night when I can during the week and every weekend."

He replied, "I miss you."

She said, "I miss you too, but remember we decided this was the best way to ensure your safety. I love you so much and could not bear it if you got hurt in my absence." Julia reminded Leo,

"You once said you could not bear the idea of having the kids find you hurt or worse."

Leo knew she was right, as always. He did not remember saying all that, but he could not argue with it. It sounded like something he'd say.

If someone had asked him right now, he'd likely say the same thing. Deep in his soul, he knew he could never go wrong by listening to Julia. She had never steered him down the wrong path, and he would always trust that and her--implicitly.

Long ago, Leo had learned that the symptoms he experienced were reason enough to doubt himself. So, when he thought he was right and Julia was wrong, he trusted it was always safer to follow her lead.

They talked a little more, and she promised to video chat with him later.

Leo couldn't help thinking, *Maybe it was just me, but every time I have to end a conversation with Julia or leave her presence, I feel a little bit lost.*

It's as though all the happiness got extracted from the room on her departure.

LEO CONSIDERED Julia the epitome of a strong woman. Yet, she had the softest core a person could have.

She grew up in a very rough neighborhood. Raised in a family whose culture purported to frown on any appearance of weakness —further hardened by a lifetime of surviving exposure to the male-dominated world.

It was Leo's experience that Julia had earned the respect of her peers for the honorable warrior she was inside. She spent more than two decades working in one of the last bastions of macho professionalism--the military-industrial complex.

She had to fight tooth and nail to overcome ignorance. Only finding increased struggle as a result of her beautiful outer shell. It sickened him.

Leo knew that it was not easy, and in those days, for all women in general. Julia had to contend with what he'd call 'Men living in the past that should not have been.'

He was always proud of how she'd excelled in the face of those hurdles. She had been part of the struggle that paved the way for today's young women. She didn't do it for accolades or recognition. It was a mix of survival and standing up for what's right.

Strong as Julia was, sometimes seeing Leo deteriorate was more than she could bear. In recent years, his dependence on her had increased in their everyday life.

His condition reached a point where his emotional age was unpredictable at times. On the surface, Leo would often seem like his normal self. Yet, it did not require much to change that. Randomly, it would leave him unable to be without her, much like a preteen. If he was sick, he could become toddler-like on his dependence on Julia. All the while, Leo went about his day as though nothing was wrong because he was, in his own way, oblivious to the changes.

In the end, he became glued to her hip.

A PRICELESS GIFT

Watching his favorite shows served several functions for Leo. In many ways, it was a form of therapy. A fact in which Leo would surely find both irony and sarcasm--because in his youth, he was outside all the time.

Yet today, his shows provided him a distraction from all the things he could no longer do. They would often provide outlets in the absence of those things which filled an average person's day.

Some shows allowed him to time travel to his childhood, while others allowed him to explore what could have been. Part of the reason Leo gravitated toward the shows he did was their inherent ability to send his unique mind on a deeply meaningful journey each time.

Julia was the first to admit she did not see what Leo saw, but she grew to enjoy his shows with him over the years. His shows were one of the few things that would bring him alive. They helped prompt a lot of talking on his better days.

Over time, he finally reached a tipping point. Leo was not gone, but Julia's health and her age required her to reconsider her plan. Leo's need for specialized care forced her to return to work. It was unavoidable if she wanted to maintain the family's lifestyle and finances.

The decision to move Leo to 'The Mountain' was long and difficult, but she and her children agreed. It was the best choice, and they all knew Leo would support them 100 percent.

The opportunity to send him there was a stroke of luck. The Mountain was an extraordinary place. So much so that occupancy is an invitation-only policy. A policy born from limited and privately donated resources.

Julia could not believe her luck when she was first approached about this special place. It turned out that Leo had made a friend in recent years who knew about his condition. They also knew he'd reached a need for a higher level of care.

The short version was Julia had been contacted by a law firm. They arranged a tour and meeting with the staff. Informing her that an anonymous friend nominated Leo for admittance to The Mountain.

Julia listened as the staff explained the history and purpose of The Mountain. Here Leo would be able to write and engage in profound, meaningful discourse. This would not be the kind of place that simply kept people safe and quiet until they crossed the rim.

It HURT Julia that the man she met so long ago had become a hollow version of who he was. So very far from the man, he could have become. The Mountain provided Julia with an option she would never have had otherwise. She and the children were grateful to Leo's anonymous benefactor.

Julia had always enjoyed his mature and solemn nature.

Leo was much younger than the men she would have typically dated. Yet, she noted he did not seem driven by egotistical male stereotypes. Leo was not concerned about how the other men viewed him. At least not where it involved machismo.

For a man of his young age, he seemed to lack any propensity for aggression or need to 'beat his chest.' He viewed women as equals in all areas; he'd even find women superior or better suited in some areas.

Leo was vocal about the duality of men.

"How could men treat women one way but expect something else for their mothers and loved ones?" he'd say.

Leo was tired of men who felt superior to women. A feeling that disappeared when the cold or flu got ahold of them. "The true hypocrites," he'd say.

When it came to certain topics of discussion, Leo would say, "My opinion is that I do not get an opinion." He believed that since he would never menstruate--why should his opinion be of any real consequence. Many men in his experience knew next to nothing about 'getting a period.' Yet, they had loads of opinions on the topic. Not the kind of guys Leo would ever hang out with.

It may sound unlikely, but this was the core of the man Julia had grown to know and love. Inside he was this and more, but inside had also changed over the years. Leo had become the first victim of his illness.

Julia appreciated that Leo only had goals to better himself and his situation. He worked in his off time toward having more options--for himself and his family.

As she got to know him better, she learned that Leo was a family man and not a party guy. He may have been college-aged, but he thought like an experienced professional. He strived to provide a good life for a wife and family.

It was the illness that would, over time, keep him from completing his college degree.

Leo had only a few classes toward completing his bachelor's degree. The bitter truth is that his dream of graduate-level studies was now nothing more than fantasy.

Julia saw great potential in Leo. Yet, she also realized that while being the smartest guy in the room, he was also too trusting and sweet for his own good. She would not say Leo was naive, but he did look to the better nature of people in the absence of reasons not to.

Before she knew it, Julia had fallen hard for Leo.

Their life was far from the epic romance it could have been. Their struggles with his health took a heavy toll on their marriage. These days when she visits, he seems oblivious to all the bad times.

He was always a gentleman who worshipped her like she was fresh from the mold. Julia could not even keep him mad at her for more than a few minutes, and that wasn't because of his illness. He was that way from the moment they met. She had to admit it was infuriating at times.

In truth, Julia could not say for sure if he was her 'One True Love' or her 'Soul Mate'--at least not in the traditional sense. It was entirely possible that Leo was neither. The thing about that was Leo knew this and worshipped her anyways.

His views on love and relationships had simple foundations.

Leo believed that love was an individual undertaking. He felt it was one of the reasons people had such a difficult time.

Leo explained that in his experience, one could only decide their love for someone else. Love does not need the return of the same to be valid--that is not true love.

Leo suggested infatuation is more likely. In his estimation, real love maintains two unmistakable qualities. The first is that love is involuntary. Some might even say it has a serendipitous quality.

The second attribute of love is an honest and deep-connecting love that is unbreakable. It does not fade or go away. Just because you can't make a relationship work shouldn't determine love's truth.

Leo would be the first to admit even the strongest and deepest love can change and even whither. Yet, as any scientist can confirm, energy can neither be created nor destroyed. It can be modified, harnessed, redirected, etc.

In Leo's view, love was energy tied directly to our life's energy. The rope between the two, while frequently ignored, is so strong that it serves to shape the sort of person we become. Our relationship to love, our own capacity for love--the love we receive from another helps determine the course of our lives in so many areas.

Some might have found this to be a weakness, but he would argue it was a strength. Leo was not a pushover exactly, but he hated seeing Julia upset for any reason. He'd always assumed that somehow, he was responsible for whatever led them down this path.

Julia always found it riveting to hear Leo talk about the issues of the day. He had a way with words that reminded her of what would be his wasted potential. Nowadays, television has become a small blessing.

BEFORE LONG, Leo was brought out of this science fiction travels by one of those rogue episodes. You know the ones. Anyone who has ever followed a favorite series can tell you there is almost always an episode you'd rather skip. This was one such episode.

With Julia's impeccable timing, Leo's phone rang, distracting him from his television show.

Leo's excitement washed away everything else, and he eagerly swiped at his phone. Despite everything, his basic need for her approval showed its face now and again.

There she was. Julia. The face that served as the sun of his universe for as long as he could remember.

The next forty minutes seemed to blow right on by. All the while, he felt like time was standing still. Julia went on about her day, the children, and her work. On good days, Leo asked the necessary questions.

In the face of his difficulties communicating, Leo spared no effort to ensure Julia knew he was interested in her life and cared about her thoughts.

He used to say, "I can't make her love me, but I can certainly remind her of my love for her."

Unfortunately, the time had come, though not unexpected, Leo asked the torturous question.

"When are you coming?"

Julia replied, "Honey, do you remember the young woman you mentioned coming by today?"

"I think so," Leo replied, "but I don't remember her name."

Julia said, "Her name is Nova Runkel, and she is your granddaughter. I know names and faces can be hard, but I wanted you to know she is coming by in a while. I asked her to bring you a poster to help with this. It has my picture and name at the top with many other names and faces. She will post it near the door to help prevent confusion; it will have under my name and face 'Visitors Approved by Julia.'"

She continued, "You will see below the names and faces of everyone you can be sure I've already spoken to about their visit. I am aware of their visit and its purpose."

Prompted in part by his paranoia, Leo asked, "What if they try to come without calling you? I don't want to get tricked."

"Do not worry, my darling," she replied. "No one can even enter the ranch without a stated visitor and, in your case, my approval. So, if they are there, I know about it. In fact," she continued, "one of the reasons Nova took a job there was to ensure she'd always be close by just in case. You may not remember this, but you two were always so close. When she was little, she used to say she was going to marry you. Though, I'm not so sure she understood the concept." Julia smiled at the recollections. "She has been caring for you since she was old enough to understand your health. You can trust Nova."

Responding with a bit of clarity, Leo said, "Aw, now I understand the tears. I feel bad I didn't even recognize her. When is Buttercup coming back? I have to apologize."

Julia assured him Nova would be there shortly with the poster. "She will be there soon," Julia said.

Julia told him it was time for his medication soon. "Baby, go pour yourself a glass of milk and get out the Ovaltine. She will be there momentarily," Julia said, "I'll be there in the morning for our coffee."

As they hung up, Julia smiled at him and said, "If you need me, just close your eyes. I love you."

CHAPTER
FIVE

A MOMENT IN TIME

It's everything I dreamed, Leo thought. He'd have finally reached what he called his Plateau of Peace.

That place where you've achieved what you set out to and are financially comfortable where the basics of life are concerned. That mystical place where you could comfortably not work and focus on your other ambitions.

I finally understand who I am and what my purpose is, he thought.

Peering out the window onto the backyard, he could see his family enjoying the comforts of their new home. The kids were in the in-ground pool. They were enjoying the sunshine with their friends. The dogs were enjoying all the visitors while making sure no random food was left on the grounds.

Leo saw his wife shuttling back and forth from the kitchen with snacks for the youngsters burning their energy as fast as she could bring out more food.

It's true; youth really is wasted on the young.

On her breaks, his wife would fuss with her flowerpots and backyard decorations. She found peace out there.

Spinning around in his chair, Leo scanned the room.

It was a moderately large office. Not luxurious, but neither was it budget friendly. His office seemed to have everything he'd always wanted.

Books, lots of books, all cataloged and lined on the wall of bookshelves. The room itself was more of a library, and the wall of shelves had a ladder that rolled back and forth. There were a lot of books, and he would find time to read and reread every one.

On the other wall, there were blackboards. Each board was littered with notes and tidbits, all related to one theory or another. Framed posters and antique maps filled the gaps.

The corner of the room was devoted to video games. It was Leos's idea of the perfect nerd cave. Sprinkled heavily with photos from all periods of his life. Memories that he always wanted in his face as he went about his pondering.

At that moment, he felt like the man he had promised Julia she was getting. A feeling he had not felt for a very long time. That feeling one gets when they can more than adequately provide for a family. There is no alternative to this feeling.

His only concern was figuring out what she was saying and doing his best to meet her needs. Some might suggest he was 'whipped.' A juvenile description, but not entirely inaccurate, and without a doubt, voluntary.

In truth, his devotion to her would appear both extreme and maybe even a little submissive to many. Leo had long ago decided he would be his own man. The stereotypes of the world would not restrict him.

With that said, accepting his reality and limitations was grueling and long. For people like Leo, successfully making it another day was the goal. No better than yesterday--the goal was no worse. For that, he'd have to see what the day brings.

Leo understood at this point that the happiness he sought wouldn't just show up. He would have to spend the day looking for the signs.

The signs weren't all that difficult. If his precious Julia was smiling, he merely needed to keep from ruining it. It had been a quarter of a century, and to him, she was no different than the first moment he laid eyes on her.

It was one of the few memories that would be with Leo for the duration. He remembers it like it was yesterday.

It was a Friday. The first week of May.

He'd spent the day checking in for a professional seminar. It was around four o'clock in the afternoon, and they had just been released for the day.

It was a beautiful afternoon in the south. The sun was shining, and there was a slight breeze. It was shaping up to be a relaxing weekend.

Leo would be there for several months and was looking forward to the break from the norm. New place, fresh faces, and some professional learning. He enjoyed this type of environment.

Leo was focused on his career, and it was going well. The recommendation for this seminar was a huge accomplishment career-wise.

Now, Leo was a smoker, and in those days, the smoking area could be a little crowded. He was waiting for a friend when something happened.

Someone had tapped his shoulder. "Excuse me." He heard. It wasn't a loud voice; it was soft, yet somehow it stood out as if there were only two people in the room. Leo turned at what felt like the slowest possible speed toward the voice.

Just then, his friend Henry said, "Hey, do you want to go?" Leo had just met Henry, another student in the seminar.

"What?" he asked.

Henry said, "What's got you so … whatever, there is a festival going on. Do you want to go?"

"Sure," Leo replied. "Let me change after we check-in, and I'll go."

A few hours later, Leo was sitting with Henry at a picnic table when he saw her again. His mystery woman was walking around with a friend. Even out of her professional clothes, she was equally as stunning. She had on jeans with little shapes cut out along her legs, accentuating her figure.

Henry was going on about something as Leo's attention was elsewhere. "You like her, huh?" Henry asked.

"Magnificent!" was the only response Leo could muster, until Henry said, "Want to meet her?"

Leo looked shocked. "You know her?" Leo asked Henry.

Henry teased Leo a bit, then said, "Yes, I know her. We work at the same office. She gave me a ride up here."

Leo didn't know what to say. He didn't have to wait long to find out. While he was processing this new information, Henry was waving her and her friend over. Leo just sat there, smoking a cigarette, trying to look calm and unmoved.

That was the moment--the one above all others. That instance, when you can feel in your heart that your life will never be the same.

Henry says, "Leo, this is my friend Julia. Julia, this is my new friend, Leo."

Staring into Julia's eyes once more, Leo found himself speechless. The only word Leo could find was "Hi."

Julia smiled and said, "Donna, if you and Henry can't behave yourselves, Leo and I are going to keep walking."

Donna replied with a smirk on her face, "I don't like you, anyways. Go on. Git!"

Leo was ready to follow Julia anywhere, and he wanted to know everything about her.

As he and Julia walked away, Donna yelled out, "Julia, make sure you bring him tonight." Julia just waved at her friend.

Turning to Leo, Julia said, "So think you'd like to go dancing tonight and maybe grab a drink?"

Leo replied, "Are you asking me on a date?"

She later admitted to Leo that she was trying to come off as confident when she replied, "Don't get ahead of yourself. It's just a few friends going as a group. Henry will fill you in if you want to go."

Did I want to go? Leo thought. *You bet your one-of-a-kind God-given Gluteus Maximus I want to go. Even if just to hear you talk and watch you dance.* What came out was, "Cool, I'll stop by."

Leo didn't know that night would be their first kiss, their first dance, and a nightlong conversation that would result in a life-long bonding that even death could not break.

CHAPTER
SIX

BABY STEPS

Decades later, she was still proving him right.

True to Julia's word, Nova showed up not a few minutes later. She had with her the poster Julia mentioned. Nova also brought Leo's medication and a small box of cocoa pebbles. It was Leo's favorite cereal. Hers too, but only because they used to eat it together.

Fixing them two bowls, Nova handed Leo a bowl and sat with him on the couch. They exchanged very few words while watching one of his favorite shows.

When Nova was younger, she discovered she could learn a great deal about her Pop by staying close. She enjoyed sharing his joys and listening to him talk about any random topic.

The thing that always stuck with her was Leo's concern for Julia. His condition didn't even lift his concern. He was always asking about her grandma.

He'd say, "What am I going to do?" Today was no different.

Nova asked, "What do you mean?"

He replied, "How do I take care of her when I'm gone?"

Nova was perplexed by the contradictory nature of his statement. His condition made so many things challenging for him.

Some were now outside the range of his abilities, but his love for Julia would not be denied.

Since she was little, she'd always hoped she would meet a man like her Pop. Someone who'd love her like he loved her Grandma Julia--unconditionally.

He once told her, "Always remember my Buttercup, anyone who places conditions on your relationship lacks a true understanding of unconditional. Always be upfront before saying yes. Love requires you to always be prepared for rejection."

"Unconditional is only achieved through honesty. If you are contemplating marriage, be sure your special someone knows who you are and ask for the same. No one short of that is worthy of you."

Tonight was a little different.

After the cereal was gone and the show was over, Leo turned to Nova and said, "Buttercup, could you do Grandpa a favor? I know exactly what to do."

On the edge of her seat, she replied, "Anything Pop, just name it." Nova meant it. It was these moments of normalcy that she longed for.

"Can you find me your grandma's friend, Donna's, phone number? I think I'm gonna need her help."

"Of course I can. Can I ask what it's for?" She inquired as she moved to the kitchen with their empty bowls.

It was the first time he'd spent any real time with Nova in recent history, or so he thought. What mattered was that he had finally learned.

He had learned how to handle the question that had weighed on him for so long.

How can he help Julia after he's gone? Who will she talk to when he's not there? He was glad it was Nova who would help him with this. Her Grandma would be extra pleased with her involvement.

A few minutes later, Nova returned, handing Leo a piece of paper.

Leo answered her question, "Well, I think I know what I'm supposed to do for my … your grandmother, but I'll need Donna's help."

She hugged him tightly goodnight. Leo walked her to the door and saw her out.

At that moment, he thought, *I am a lucky Grandpa. Life was so cruel to rob the memories of that girl from me.*

RETURNING TO THE COUCH, Leo grabbed the slip of paper and his phone. He dialed. After a few rings, a voice answered.

Leo said, "Hello. Is this Donna?"

Donna replied, "Leo, is that you? Is everything alright? Is Julia okay?"

Leo replied, "Julia is fine. Better than fine, but that will change in time. To help her, I need your help. More accurately, Julia needs your help. Can we meet?"

Donna asked, "Are you sure she's okay? Are you okay?"

Leo replied, "Honestly, I don't know how much you know about my health, but it is becoming less and less likely that I'll improve, and I could really use your help with something."

Leo knew the idea sounded preposterous but was unfazed.

He said, "Doing nothing will definitely not help her, but there is something I can do that might help her when the time comes."

This convinced Donna as much as anything else he'd said. The good news, she was on board with his plan.

OVER THE NEXT FEW WEEKS, Leo set about writing with all his free time. It was not an easy process, and he lost focus quite often. Thankfully, Nova was adept at getting her Pop up and moving.

Nova had advanced warning of his condition most of her life. She made it a point she would one day be able to help him when others could not.

She had intentionally geared her education to be able to ensure she would be able to help him when he recognized her and when he didn't.

She was a gem of a granddaughter, a woman with an ability to make someone smile every morning. Her children don't know how lucky they will be or are. Leo couldn't remember if she had kids.

Keeping Leo's confidence, she collected his writings daily as she cleaned up and stored them in a small chest. It was all a part of Leo's plan. Knowing he would fluctuate day to day, he and Nova set about ensuring this plan would come off without a hitch.

As time went on, Leo was having more bad days than good days.

On one occasion, Leo was asleep when Nova arrived but was startled awake by the sound of dishes.

"Buttercup, is that you?" Leo asked.

"Hey Pop," she replied, "How was your nap?"

"It was delightful, my darling girl. Don't suppose you brought any cereal with you?"

"Two bowls of cocoa pebbles coming right up."

Nova brought the bowls to the couch and sat down next to her Pop.

"How was your day?" Leo asked.

Nova responded, "It's great now that I'm with my favorite guy." Smiling, she kissed her Pop on the cheek and asked him, "how are you feeling today?"

"Well, to be honest, I feel surprisingly clear-headed. I don't feel the usual confusion. Just a good day, I suppose," Leo said.

Nova knew these days were few and far between, so she planned on staying as long as Pop could endure company tonight.

Taking advantage of the day, she asked him how his plan was going. "Great. I'm still writing, and everything is on track. I still depend on you to sort through and pull out the pointless nonsense I might mix in," Leo said.

Nova replied, "Pop, you don't have to worry about a thing. You found your answer, and I will help you execute your plan."

Leo was impressed with this marvelous young woman. He was proud of the legacy she represented. For some reason, his mind chose this moment to remind him of the day he convinced her parents to name her Nova. He remembered being at the hospital, holding her only moments after she was born.

Maybe it was his illness, but he could have sworn there was an unspoken connection as he stared into her eyes. She stared back, and he even caught a smile. Her eyes wide open, she appeared as happy as a baby could be.

When the nurse came in to ask the parents the name--he blurted out, "Nova--because she will make the world into something new and beautiful."

After some discussion, her parents relented, and he and Nova became as inseparable as they could be considering. It wasn't until he started to forget things that Nova became more devoted to him.

She would spend nearly all her free time visiting Pop. Nova would quietly sit with him while he watched TV, and they'd eat cereal together. It was adorable, but after a few years, there was a concern.

It was clear that Leo's condition would affect her more than most as it worsened. So naturally, there was concern that she wasn't doing all the things other kids were. She was a great student, but her only extracurricular hobby was her Pop.

It wasn't until her parents sat her down to talk that everyone realized this was precisely where Nova belonged. Leo was right. No one could explain it, but there was a connection between those two that could not be denied.

Leo remembered when Nova was twelve and had to explain to others, yet again, why she spent so much time with him.

Nova had said, "I know you are my parents and want the best for me but let me ask you a few questions. Am I correct that you want me to be happy and socialized? You want me to get good grades and land a challenging and financially rewarding career, right? To find love, real love, and have a happy, safe family life?"

To which her parents had replied, "Yes, of course. Absolutely."

Nova then informed them. "In that case, please understand that this is my plan. I intend to pursue a career in dementia counseling. It is clear to me that even those who love a person like Pop can have trouble understanding them, leading to numerous manifestations of stress and exhaustion."

Her dad had said, "Well, you certainly pay attention, don't you."

"Yes, I do, even when you don't think I am. As the saying goes, kids are like sponges, and I've learned that it can be easier for me to understand Pop sometimes better than the grownups. This is one of the things I will figure out. As for Pop, he needs me, and I can learn a lot from him. I think it will help me be better at helping other families someday."

Nova continued, "And Mom, I know you want me to find love. I promise you that I have given it serious thought, and with Pop's help, I know exactly how to find the perfect partner and when to know if the time is right. Until then, I will focus on helping Pop until I can help those like him. As Pop always says, 'Love will blossom when nature thinks it's time.' So don't worry, Mom. I have this under control."

BACK IN THE PRESENT, Leo asked Nova, "Buttercup, why do you work here? Surely you could get a better career instead of hanging around with some old man."

Nova said, "Pop, I want you to listen to me. I know you won't remember what I'm going to say, so I just want you to remember that this is my purpose."

Leo asked, "What do you mean by purpose?"

"When I was a little girl," Nova said, "we were watching TV, and I said I was bored. You said you're bored because you lack purpose. I didn't know what you meant, and you told me, 'I watch TV because I lack other things to do, so my purpose is to stay entertained until dinner. It's not a major purpose, but even no purpose can be a purpose. It's why adults sit around after work doing nothing. They intend to do nothing because they have been busy all day. The rest is intentional. In some cases, the distraction from thoughts of work is the purpose.' You told me if I stay aware of my purpose, I won't get bored. You also said I'd accomplish many things."

"It really sounds like I talk too much," Leo said with a smile.

"Pop, I then asked you how I could get started if I wanted to do something. You told me the only way to accomplish anything was baby steps. Whether a phone call, an application, or simply picking up a book. Consider your purpose and plan. After that, it was simply a matter of one step after another."

"You told me, 'Every dream can be reached via baby steps. Every step is one step closer.'" Nova told him, adding, "I took that to heart."

Leo replied, "I'm so glad I've been of some help. I hope it proves useful."

Nova couldn't resist. She hugged her Pop, knowing his time and clarity were fragile things. "Pop, I want to tell you exactly how you impacted my life. I learned from you my whole life and made it my life mission to help you and people like you. I studied to become a counselor."

Leo said, "I'm so proud of you; that's awesome. See, you should work at a hospital or doctor's office."

"No, Pop, let me finish," Nova said. "That's what I studied in college. After I finished high school, I got my real estate license. I helped people find Forever Homes while earning enough for school. The networking required eventually crossed paths with my work around dementia patients and their families. The result was this place--The Mountain."

Leo looked at her, confused, unsure of how the two connected.

Nova continued, "You know how it's invitation-only? You can never tell anyone this, but I sit on the Board of Directors for this place."

Nova explained to him, "This place--The Mountain--was created after I convinced some developers and investors that a place like this could be supported by pooling the skills and resources of caretakers."

Leo seemed to be understanding as she continued, "You see, caretakers have so many things to worry about. As well as so many expenses, that if one person can cover all the plumbing needs of a neighborhood and so on with numerous professions and skillsets of the caretakers then it could really benefit every-one. Maybe even make the caregivers' life less stressful and provide for more meaningful time to spend with endurers."

"In the end, it's merely one big subdivision where the care-takers work together to collectively make everyone's life a little better," she said.

Nova continued, "Long story short, the facts and numbers came together, so they agreed to try. The Mountain is the first of several planned residential properties."

"It was helped along by two of the CEO's who convinced the others. They were faced with their own diagnoses and convinced the rest that who you were in life doesn't matter in the least when you become an endurer." Nova said, "After explaining to them all the doctors in the world wouldn't change their lives. The Board agreed that the quality of life for an endurer needed The Moun-tain. It was agreed that the financial risk didn't negate the poten-tial benefits for themselves and their loved ones."

Nova looked at Leo and said, "You know you can't tell anyone, right, Pop?"

Leo simply replied, "Well, honey, I am certainly proud of you."

And a second later, he said, "Oh yea, do you know where the remote is?"

Nova felt the sun go down on her day with Pop. A tear rolled down her cheek as she said, "Let's check the bedroom, Pop, maybe you left it in there." She knew he didn't, but clearly, it was time for bed.

CHAPTER
SEVEN

THE PROMISE

Julia dries her tears and tries to patiently wait as Donna continues telling her about the conversation she had with Leo. She has never seen Donna struggle so much to talk; her coffee is now getting cold.

Donna starts again, "I said, 'Of course, I will be there.' He looked at me again and said, 'No, I mean, will you be there for her every day for the first few months after? Can you be completely available to Julia at a moment's notice?'" Donna says that she'd assured Leo she would be. After that, Leo made her swear to him her most sacred promise.

Tears are already falling down Julia's face again.

Donna grasps Julia's hand and gives it a squeeze before continuing, "At this point, I didn't know what to expect. I was caught completely off guard as it was, then Leo handed me a box. He said he always felt a need to write and could never put his finger on what to write. He said he was told he had a way with words for most of his life. He also said you gave him purpose."

"It was in that brief moment," Donna says, "there was a clarity about him that I had not seen in quite some time. He told me he knew in his heart that you felt the same as him, but his words and actions got in the way. Leo said it was partly his condition and partly his manly idiocracy. He also seemed very sure of something else." Donna pauses and smiles at Julia. "Girl, that man loved you, and he sure did know you."

Julia abruptly stands, clearing her throat. "Want some more coffee?" she asks.

Donna nods.

"I'm going to freshen up real quick; you shouldn't have to deal with this." Waving her hands over her disheveled appearance, Julia giggles. Honestly, she probably hasn't gone to 'freshen up' in a day or two.

Yikes. Perhaps I should start getting ahold of myself, she thought.

She reminds herself of the conversations she'd had with Leo when his days were hard.

Arriving at the bathroom, Julia gazes in the mirror, alarmed by what she sees. She can't remember the last time she looked in the mirror.

That husband of mine. Just couldn't let me sit and be depressed, she thought.

Right now, she needs to know what else Donna has to tell her, so she sets about making herself presentable-ish. Once Julia is satisfied with her appearance, she goes back to Donna.

"Okay, now get to the end quickly, or I'll have to torture it out of you." She laughs.

Donna most likely knows that Julia is now on edge. It feels nice to be excited about something again. Lately, she doubted it was even possible anymore.

Donna tries to reach for her phone to tease interruption, but Julia looks at her with a 'you'd better not' face and smiles.

"Julia, this man looked me in the eyes and--no kidding--he said ... well, why don't I just let you have a listen."

Donna grabs her phone before pressing a button and says to Julia, "I can tell you what he said if you'd rather not listen to the recordings. If it's too much, just tell me right now."

Julia's face is filled with an uncertain surprise. She asks, "What do you mean ... listen?"

Donna explains, "Well, after our conversation, Leo sent me some audio clips. Seems he recorded our conversations to help with his writing and had decided--his email said--'Julia will probably kill you if you don't have some audio of our conversation so I am sending you a few clips.' So I have a few audio clips but not the entire conversations."

"But again," Donna repeats, "If it's too much for your emotions, just say so, please."

Julia nods in agreement.

Donna then hits a few buttons, and Leo's voice fills the room. His recorded voice says,

"A few days after the situation dies down and visitors have stopped calling and coming by, and everyone goes back to their lives, the love of my life will be sitting in pain. I can't do anything to stop it, but maybe I can do something to change it. I'm guessing it'll be a weekend because she will likely have nowhere to be in a hurry. Life will have brushed away the passing as it does, leaving everyone to go about the business at hand."

Donna sees the tears begin to pool in Julia's eyes and moves to pause the recording, but Julia stops her.

Leo's voice continues,

"She will be sitting where we have our coffee and watch the news, where the smallest conversations are a reminder of who we were and what we were about. This time I won't be there. It may take a few days, but my not being there will cause her to dwell on all the what if's. Questioning whether she did her best and loved me as best she could. My Julia is the most confident and self-assured person I've ever known, but her tender heart will cause her to question herself in the aftermath. It is just how she balances the harder parts of her personality, which in turn give her the

strength she turned out to need in life. She is a masterpiece of life. She will also have to learn that she doesn't have me to talk to. As time goes on, she will feel the impact of not having me to talk to."

At this point, it is clear to Donna that Julia should take a minute. Donna stops the recording, hands Julia a tissue, and says, "Could you get me a refill?"

Julia nods and grabs her cup. She gets up and heads toward the kitchen. She looks down toward the cup but doesn't acknowledge that the cup is still half full.

She knows her friend is forcing her to take a minute, and for that, she is grateful. This is what she has wanted since he left.

The sound of Leo's voice is the answer to many recent dreams, but the price is a stinging pain. It's as though someone is jabbing long needles into her heart.

When she enters the kitchen, she puts the cup on the counter and just lets out a howl followed by what seems to be buckets of tears. She couldn't stop the flow if she wanted to.

They come like torrential rains in the spring.

Donna is there in a flash catching Julia before she can hit the ground. Julia's knees had buckled but Donna caught her friend just in time. She holds Julia in her lap and waits for her friend's expression of grief to wane.

When the tears stop, Julia holds Donna and whispers, "Thank you." Followed by a louder, "Now, let's go hear what else my hopeless romantic of a husband had in mind. Shall we?"

Donna follows Julia back to their seats, and they get comfortable. Donna sets the phone on the table, and with a look at Julia, she grabs her hand and hits play.

Leo's voice is there once again.

"On this day, because I know you will know when. She won't be answering your calls or texts. She'll be canceling work or what-

ever she has going at the time. She might even begin to isolate herself in the smallest but new manner. You are her closest friend, and I trust you will know when it is time. When that happens, give her this."

Donna pauses it.

"So, of course, I asked him what it was, what was in it," Donna states, "and this is what he said."

Donna hit play, and Leo explains,

"A long time ago, Julia told me to write stuff down. It began for various reasons, and I did try to make it work for us, but it never really did. Until now. Now that I have a concrete idea of the limited possibilities my future holds in spite of medical science, I'm going to begin my purpose of helping her through my loss."

Leo continues,

"In here will be writings that I want her to have after I pass. I want her to feel like she can still talk to me and feel like I'm still talking to her. I want to help ease her transition into the next chapter of her life. When something happens and she wonders what I would say, or maybe she stops to consider if I agree with her assessment of something. At that moment, I want to provide her a way of communicating with me. I want her to always feel the comfort of my presence without feeling intruded upon. I know it's not something she'll want to talk about, but I still feel that sense of responsibility for her after I pass. Her happiness has always been my responsibility in exchange for her love. It is my personal belief that if couples tried to focus on what made their partner happy, then the world would be filled with couples who had a balanced, fulfilled relationship. Yes, it makes you vulnerable, but if you've chosen correctly, you should notice right away if they believe likewise."

Donna watches Julia as she listens. A combination of random tears and a smile on Julia's face leaves Donna with a sense of jealousy she can't quite process. Inside, she knows that Julia had something she can only hope to one day find.

Donna hopes there is still time for her to know that mix of pleasure and pain. In some weird way, it seems to express the love she imagines the whole world is constantly searching for. Julia is both the luckiest and unluckiest person she's ever met. Hands down.

Donna remembers the conversation with Leo. It makes so much more sense to her now.

All of it comes into focus as Leo's voice continues,

"If you believe in all the teachings of balance in the universe, one can't deny that positive and negative exist in everything. Whatever you want to label it. Let's generalize and call it energy. The energy that guides your happiness and relationships is born from the energy you offer. People like to say this kind of thing all the time, but I suppose not until one faces death do you truly hear the truth in words like that. While it's certainly not a precise science, universities around this nation have classes devoted to teaching the golden rule. Still, it's always dressed up in words that shadow the importance of its application."

Julia squeezes Donna's hand and mouths the words, "Thank you."

Leo's voice is a song to Julia's ears.

"Famous philosophers have even debated its use. Everyone grasps it, and everyone will make an argument for it when it's doubted. It is rooted in nearly all systems of belief going back millennia.

With a few notable exceptions--dictators, monarchs, world lead-ers, and these days, politicians sprinkled with a few so-called celebrities--application seems to lose out more often than we consider. I noted the exceptions because those people have other issues that get in the way of living a golden rule kind of life. The question is, what is your reason for not adhering to it? Some-times it is just the question that is important, more so than the answer. Don't think so?"

Donna realizes it is time to give Julia another break, so she pauses here and says, "I was thinking as he was talking and real-ized that I had to agree with some of the things he was saying. Remember that guy in college?"

Julia does, so she nods.

Donna is referring to this guy she was so into. He was nice. He had an average appearance, and she couldn't understand why they didn't click just right. Donna always told herself she was young, and it was just one of those learning relationships, but Julia notes how his name has come up more than once over the years. Donna claims he was the one that got away, and Julia always reminds her it isn't too late.

"He was always the perfect guy for me," Donna says. "We liked the same things and enjoyed spending time together. It was effortless. He was always there for me when I needed him, and while he was a guy who sometimes did annoying guy things, he was great. I suppose I saw him more as a friend because he still hadn't given me butterflies. Things with him were nice, though. I always felt safe, comfortable, and our sex life was healthy. It just seemed like something was missing. He wasn't enough like the guy on the poster. Do you remember the poster?" Donna asks.

She does remember the poster. Julia doesn't remember the name of the guy on the poster, but he was hot and chiseled, some-thing Donna's friend from college wasn't. Donna, being Donna, would always tell Julia how the guy in the poster was her fantasy guy. Someone who could just make her weak in the knees at the sight. Just the usual fantasy-related adolescent predictions of their future.

Donna continues, "I know I was young, and perhaps my juvenile notions about how my husband should be were more damaging than I thought. If I'm honest with myself, had he looked closer to my ideal image of a hunk, I probably would have felt more passionate about the idea of being with him. In turn, maybe I would have treated him differently. He was kind of perfect. Do you think that perhaps in some subconscious way, my mind wanted him, but my body couldn't let go and give in to passion in some way based on what my eyes saw?"

"We'll talk about David later, but yes, I do." With a smirk and a wink, Julia says, "My dearest friend, Donna, please continue with your story about my Leo before I resort to physical reminders."

Through faux fear, Donna replies, "Okay, okay, but we will return to David." As Donna reaches for a cookie, she says, "You'd better get a new box of tissues before I tell you the next part."

Julia grabs a new box and suggests they move to the living room. The living room is modest, bright, and open. She and Leo had always shared a love of open, welcoming spaces in their home.

The living room was a comfortable place for Leo despite struggling to sit still and enjoy himself. Although he never spent long periods of time there, he had told Julia that she'd made it the center of their welcoming home.

Plunking down on the couch, Donna asks, "So was Leo always a hopeless romantic?"

"Why do you say that? You know what he was like with the flowers and gestures."

"Well, the conversation I had with Leo has me questioning my choices with David. Although, I'm thinking he somehow planned that." Donna giggles a little bit. "I always knew you had a weird one, but like you, no one understood exactly why."

"Hey, my Leo was not … okay a little bit. But he was sweet,

caring, and lived only in the best moments of our lives. It was maddening. Only I get to call him weird. In many ways, it was both a blessing and a curse for us, but mostly for him," Julia says.

"Darling, I'm not sure exactly how you managed all these years. To this day, I'm honestly not sure if I could do it," Donna says.

Julia can only bow her head at the memory of the weight of it all. The memory of which still catches her at moments where she must adjust to a sudden lightness of that weight. Julia knows it is all temporary, but admittedly, part of her is content for it never to end if it means keeping him with her. The mix of relief and sorrow seems never-ending and always leaves her feeling guilty somehow.

Donna, still talking, says, "But something I learned from you over the years is how love is what keeps you going. There is love, deep and pure, romantic, and intimate. Then there is unconditional love. I guess what I'm saying is that my experience as your best friend leaves me no doubt that you love this man. You love him like no other person on earth. Despite his many involuntary flaws, you never lost sight of the man you married and the potential he had. I've seen you struggle over the years with this entire concept. You've seen him do and say things that are not like him. You had found a way to absorb that your Leo was trapped. Something that many can't seem to do. As Leo would describe it, he was trapped inside of a vehicle with faulty engineering and no way out. Sometimes with close attention, one can see the signs that he was still in there.

"This I've learned from you, and I'm grateful to have been your friend and shared your journey in some small way. It's made me a better person, or as Leo would say, 'The experience has helped me grow into a better me.'"

They laugh at her sarcastic approach to his words. He and Donna used to have exchanges like that all the time.

He would usually walk away, saying, "You'll see. One day both of you will see."

Laughing with Donna, Julia says, "You'll see. One day both of you will see."

In that moment, where laughter and the bladder argue, Julia realizes Leo is no doubt smiling at them--wherever he may be.

As Donna runs off to the bathroom, she can hear Leo—

"Life will move on, and you will laugh again. Enjoy it, for you may not get another chance."

That husband of hers had no doubt planned this.

Returning from the bathroom, Donna says, "Okay, now I have to tell you a little something about the box."

REFLECTION

It suddenly feels serious as Donna sits down. "Leo suggested you might be irked but in the end would appreciate this part.

"All the while I've been here, I have been laying down clues. He suggested it was a game you played with the kids. At the end of the clues, you will find the key," Donna reveals. "He was very specific about where to put them and said the box isn't fortified, but the hunt would make it meaningful. Though, he promised he would only do it for the first one. I convinced him that it was not romantic but a nuisance."

Julia mouths the words, "Thank you."

Even from beyond the rim, Leo is still trying to make her life better, albeit in his own quirky but kind-hearted way.

"Wait!" Julia says in a stern and serious voice, "He wanted the contents to be a secret?"

"Oh no," Donna says. "What Leo wanted was to infuse it with memories. He wanted to help but also remind you of the good times. Leo wanted me to explain that inside the box awaited your conversations." She giggles a bit and says, "He told me you'd be pleased you only had to talk to him when you wanted to now. It made him giggle."

Julia smiles, grabbing another tissue.

Now, this was more like her Leo. He was terrible with surprises. Julia couldn't recall Leo ever making it to Christmas or her birthday without telling her in advance what she was getting. He literally couldn't wait to make her happy. Julia was sure it was all an early symptom masked as behavior, but it still made things fun, especially once they started having kids. In fact, Leo protested every conversation regarding the proper age for the Santa discussion. In Leo's perfect world, everyone would believe in Santa their whole lives.

He could never wait for the kids to get up on Christmas morning. He was also so noisy. Stomping around in the kitchen. Clumsily opening the doors to their rooms to see if they were up. At one point, Julia had to sternly urge him to leave the kids alone and quietly watch TV until they woke on their own.

If she had left it up to Leo, he would undoubtedly let the kids open half of their presents before they went to bed the night before.

Donna says, "He worried that when he was gone, you would avoid reflection, that it'd be too easy to find solace in your isolation. Are you ready for more?"

Julia nods.

Donna hits play, and Leo's voice fills the living room for the first time in what seemed to Julia like forever.

Leo says,

"I will never find peace if I leave her to find a new path alone. Don't you see? I am supposed to be her best friend. I've never understood the idea that her being my wife meant anything more than she was my best friend for life."

"Best friends who have committed to living life together. Sometimes you don't even share addresses. If you are lucky, you will

survive the expectations and beliefs of others. I don't wish this on you, but life may one day bring dark clouds your way."

Leo continues,

"When grieving, some will make snap decisions almost always due to the expectations of others. Some will contemplate for a bit or express their anger/disappointment. The pensive types will likely ask lots of questions before knowing how to proceed."

"Very few will reach the point of considering how to move forward. That's a tough one right there. These people are likely more in tune with their own mistakes."

"In the end, decisions will have to be considered and later made but making them together helps to fortify them against the future. This leaves the big question. How did they do it? How are they still together? Well, that is the most complicated question of all and also the simplest."

"Love is the simple part. If you have no love, then don't lie to each other nor yourself. Make peace, forgive for yourself and for them."

DONNA TAKES a minute to ensure Julia is still okay to hear more, but before she can hit the pause button, Julia smacks her hand. She got her answer.

LEO CARRIES ON,

"You may find negative feelings to be the proper response, but it's also the expected one. Take the high road if for no other reason

than to withdraw from the situation with grace. It helps that they wonder why you didn't react as expected. For some, they will ponder the cost and whether they let the one get away."

"Whatever your reason or, in this case, their reasons, they opted to find a fix that made their continued journey possible. Two people committed to traveling the path of life together. The adjustments or allowances made in relationships are the business of the couple. People will always give you advice. Don't let their voices take part in the decision-making."

"Should this occur, you will learn new things about each other. Some good, some not so good, but your love should not change. Surviving these clouds together will only strengthen your resolve to face the next ones that come."

"This is why I feel that my absence is no excuse for not at least trying to help guide her. I must also try for our babies. You are now her best friend, and this is the only way I can pass on the torch. Please say you understand."

DONNA HITS PAUSE AND SAYS, "Honey, at this point, I was too stunned to cry. It has been my experience that men don't have the depth for that kind of love. You are very lucky to have experienced that kind of love for any period in your life. I'd suggest at this point you play his game and see where it takes you."

Julia laughs.

Donna asks, "Why do you laugh? I'm being serious here. For a brief moment, I felt the love he had for you … sorry, still has for you. It was an intense feeling, but it also explained the tension I've seen over the years between you two. I mean, every couple has issues, but the love you showed each other didn't fit with the tension I'd noticed."

"I asked him," she continues, "if he was always like this, and he laughed." Donna grabs her phone and says, "Leo explained in his own words." Fumbling with her phone, she hits play, saying, "Give me a tissue for this one."

LEO'S VOICE RETURNS,

"The only way I can describe my love for her is to explain that Julia taught me about true unconditional love. Once I understood that it was easy. I found the feelings I had for her in the beginning and held on to them no matter what came our way or even how ugly things might have gotten during low periods. I do what I can to enhance her life. I try to make as few mistakes as possible along the way. Meanwhile, I put my faith in the love I have for her and hoped I could inspire her to focus her love on me. That's all I can really do."

"You know how my gears are out of whack causing me to do and say things I might not normally say?"

You can hear Donna reply, "Of Course."

LEO SAYS,

"Well, reverse it. Think of the last time you dealt with a stressful situation. It could be the death of a loved one, a major disappointment in your career, or maybe just a breakup. You will always hear--oh, that's a perfectly natural feeling. The details don't matter. Every situation might be different, but people always tell you what you are feeling is natural. Well, there are many things natural to a caretaker's life that they have to overcome. Unfortunately, that rarely comes before understanding the source of the behavior."

"Human beings are just built that way. If I can't understand this inherent flaw in her, how can I expect her to understand it in me? It is reflection that guides one to overcoming their engineering."

THE AUDIO CLIP ENDS. All Julia can do is reach for more tissues.

Turning to Donna and shaking her finger, Julia says, "Reflection. You'll see. One day both of you will see."

They both laugh as Julia sarcastically does a Leo impersonation.

Julia says, "Leo always hoped he'd find a way to teach others what he'd learned, but his illness made simple conversations challenging. Given his skill at writing, I suggested he write things down. I encouraged him to write short stories. Unfortunately, I didn't think he took me seriously or ever finished them."

"Oh, my dear girl, you have some reading in store for you," Donna says.

CHAPTER
NINE

AGAIN?

"**F**racking Hell!" Julia blurts out. It is one of the most annoying things she has going on at the moment. "Sorry about that," she tells Donna.

"What do you mean?" Donna asks.

Julia explains, "That noise, don't you hear it? Every night they want to play their loud music. All the ruckus from the dancing and carrying on. I swear I can't hear myself think sometimes."

Donna stares at her for a moment. Then she asks Julia, "You mean from the Miller's place?"

The Miller family has lived down the road from Leo and Julia for many years. 'Friends' may be a bit of a stretch, but they have exchanged conversations in passing for much of that time. Bobby Miller Jr. and his wife, Barbara-Lee, are kind, friendly neighbors. They were warm and welcoming when Leo and Julia moved in.

It's never easy moving to a new home. Julia and Leo were excited, even hopeful for their new place. Having searched through different properties, finding one that had the perfect neighborhood proved difficult.

For Leo and Julia, their home had to be a place they retreated to for safety. A sacred temple to prepare their children for the world, and when the seasons of child-rearing faded, it would be a home that would safeguard the memories of yesterday and their future memories.

Neither of them had family within a day's drive from the house, but they had each other--just the two of them against the world.

For both of them, their place of birth and upbringing was not what they wanted in life. Nor was it what they wanted for their children.

They planned on having several children and wanted, as all parents do, the best environment. For them, this was a small to medium-sized town. Mostly rural with the big city conveniences that make small-town life easier.

While they never really became socially involved, Bobby and 'Babs,' as her friends called her, were instrumental to their settling experience. Babs took Julia on a tour of the area and the town to acclimate her to everything she might need. Bobby did the same for Leo.

Leo spoke to Bobby more often than Julia spoke to Babs. Aside from the children, Julia and Babs only ever talked about gardens and food recipes. Bobby would catch Leo outside smoking from time to time and just chit-chat about little things.

Somewhere along the line, Leo shared an idea he had for Bobby's backyard. Leo liked their property, mainly because it was twice the size of their plot; half was wooded.

Leo told him how, if he'd had the extra space, he would've built a kind of sanctuary in the center.

Leo was never comfortable with the notion of others watching him when he was in the backyard. Given the cost of privacy fencing, he simply had to make do with what they could.

Julia tells Donna, "He'd always say 'If I were Bobby ...' He had the idea of building a small building in the center of the wooded lot. He'd clear out a space to build a 'he-shed' in the center, and a small road would lead in and out, so they could drive a golf cart from the back door to the he-shed. The idea was more complex, but I never really paid attention."

"Explain to me why this has you riled up?" Donna asks. "Is this related to that noise we keep hearing?"

Julia clarifies, "Sorry, yes, it has everything to do with it. Men are fickle. See, they might not have been close friends, but Bobby decided that after Leo passed, he would build Leo's idea. Bobby calls it a dedication to Leo's struggles. I think he's using emotion to get one over on Babs and build his he-shed in the process.

"The point being," Julia continues, "Bobby comes home after work each night and runs his loud equipment. I can't wait until he retires in a few months. Then he can work on it during the day."

Donna comments, "Now that I understand your little outburst, I'm going to guess that means it's getting late."

JULIA AND DONNA have talked and cried for hours.

Julia remembers how Leo used to pretend to be *that* guy. He would pretend to be all forceful, 'putting his foot down.' It was a riot. Leo just did it to make her smile, but they both knew that was not a persona he could pull off. Some might call him soft, but she learned it was just his creamy caramel center. Leo would do, agree to, go along with … almost anything if he thought Julia truly needed it or wanted it and just asked for it.

Julia says, "Leo used to say, 'You can be proud or married, but you can't always be both.' People weren't sure how to take him when he said that. He said it was easier to explain to younger men because they were less tainted."

Donna asks, "What did he mean by tainted? That sounds contagious."

Julia just laughs. She had thought the same thing when Leo said it. "No, not like a disease. Well, not really." Julia further explains that Leo believed growing up had good and bad influences on young men, and those were often overlooked. One such area is where relationships are concerned.

"Remember when Leo was talking about a woman's caution?" Julia asks. Donna nods, so Julia explains to Donna that Leo's views were unconventional at best, and Leo knew it. He knew his ideas and notion about life were unlikely to catch on. He'd say, 'It's not like I believe anything that hasn't been said already. Pretty sure no one else really has either. Perspective and application are the keys. It seems death provides a kind of clarity that only comes when approaching the rim.'

"Kinda dark, right?" Julia says. "He was always saying things like that. I teased him that he fancied himself an oracle, and he'd reply, 'Oracle's are historically women. Besides, everyone knows what I know. They just haven't noticed yet. They are too busy listening to everyone else. So much energy is spent on the opinions of others, they'll come around. You'll see.'"

Giggling, Donna says, "You'll see. One day both of you will see." After they laugh, Donna asks, "Is that why he didn't like David?"

Julia hesitantly replies, "Well, kind of. You see, growing up, Leo was always different. He was always an outsider walking the edge as his peers grew."

"How do you mean?"

Julia takes a deep breath as though she is about to explain something she had explained a million times. This is because, in a manner of speaking, she has. As Leo got worse, she, like most caregivers, had been subject to receptively explaining the deeper source of some of her endurers' behaviors. Sadly, his siblings were often the ones who needed educating on their own brother.

Julia tells Donna, "He always had friends around. He was always part of a group; he just didn't have any close friends. All the social groups in his school were relative to a sport or activity. As he entered high school, and those youth activities dwindled, he realized the only real social circle he had were the neighborhood kids. They were all good friends, and he'd known them most of his life.

"He just never quite fit in. When I asked him once why, he'd say, 'I wasn't man enough.' Of course, I told him that was nonsense. I didn't want to overdo it because, well, you know."

Donna says, "You mean because he wasn't really 'manly.'"

Julia musters the appearance of insult and says, "Well, I didn't want to say it, but I suppose he didn't check all the boxes of the stereotype."

"He was a wonderful man Julia. It doesn't matter," Donna says.

Julia, with a tear in her eye, replies, "I know it doesn't matter. It never mattered, but he just didn't seem to believe that."

Donna asks, "What do you mean? He didn't think he was man enough?"

Julia explains, "See, that was the problem as Leo saw it. His rational mind had no concern for the thoughts of others. He was confident, secure, and not the least bit jealous. Okay, well, maybe a little, but not in the possessive fashion. His worries always rested on what I thought of him and how close it was to what I needed.

"As a young man, he was sensitive and intellectual. Not two traits boys look for in friends. It was his experience that young ladies didn't care much for those traits either. Now, he drew his share of female attention as he aged, but keeping it, proved more difficult."

Julia continues, "His problem as he'd tell it was all the archaic notions that filled his head from fathers, uncles, etc. The male role models of the world and even the images on the screen. They all told him he had to be some big, strong, take-no-crap kind of guy. All brawn--brains if there's room. Yet, the only things worthy of a guy's brain power were his job, cars, guns, girls, and of course, the all-powerful money ... no wait, money is number 3. Power and ego are 1 and 2. Fame was mixed in there somewhere, and ladies have no number because it is simple 1, ladies, 2, ladies, 3, lad- ... you get the picture.

"Through it all, Leo got the idea that he wanted to be a one-woman guy. Contrary to the advice and expectations from the men in his orbit, Leo did not have a desire to bed every woman he met. He wanted something more from a relationship.

"He wanted a huge family and a respectable but intellectually challenging profession. He wanted to be the kind of husband a wife would always be proud of. A man she could rely on at all times. One who never left her to feel neglected or unappreciated. Leo wanted to be the kind of man who worked hard but always had time for his wife. He'd always have time to watch the kids so she could rest or tend to other things.

"Leo wanted his wife to have girlfriends and an active social life. At least that's what the stereotypes taught him."

Julia pauses a minute to grab a tissue and dab her tears. They are slow but steady.

Donna grabs her friend's hand and says, "Take your time. I already called in sick for tomorrow."

Julia laughs and says, "Did you tell them your friend's husband just passed, and you need to help her with something?"

Donna breaks out in laughter, "Girl, I've been helping you for months now."

The laughter ensues, and Julia says, "I hope I wasn't too much of a bother taking you away from work."

"I'm your best friend; you know I'll always be there for you." Then with a smirk, Donna adds, "It's no trouble. I get the days off with pay."

"You are incorrigible," Julia says, which is true. However, Julia knows Donna is joking. Donna is not that kind of risk-taker. As a single woman, her job means everything to her.

"Okay," Donna says, "Finish telling me why he thought so little of himself."

"Actually, Leo would argue that he didn't think little of himself. He was simply accepting individual facts. For example, if he said no one wants to be his friend, one could say that's not true because he knew so many people. Yet, Leo would argue it was true because, of all those great many people he knew, no one called on his birthday, not even siblings. No one ever stopped by to see what he was up to, and his list would continue. In that way, I suppose he was right.

"People knew him, but they never saw him as a guy to hang with even early on. He was the go-to guy at work. Leo was the one to go to with questions or help in finding something. He gave great advice and knew a lot about a lot of things. Yet, in all the years we've been married, no one ever called or came by just because they wanted to connect. There was always an 'I wanted to ask you,' 'Have you ever heard,' 'Do you know,' 'Can I borrow,' … you can imagine the variety over the years.

"Over the years, no one ever just brought over a video game, some beers, or a book--no other agenda than to talk and hang out. It's been this way since his youth.

"Something else you might not know about him. Leo was picked on in his youth for being different. Different name, pigment, interests, skills. He played sports his entire childhood but was only good at one of them.

"He never pretended to be what he wasn't, and in the end, he never quite measured up. People loved him just fine. He'd be welcome to parties and social events, but they didn't go out of their way to invite him.

"The first girl he ever asked to dance told him she couldn't because he was too different. That's when he started to take notice. She was right. He began noticing the comments and glances. The insults were dressed up in humor. As he got older, and girls took a more significant role in his thoughts, he noticed other things. He'd often be called handsome and attractive. He'd been told he was funny, kind, and even a good listener. He wasn't a pale-skinned jock who brought the center of attention to him —*that* guy who had a great physique and maybe a car.

"Most of the girls who he had his first relationships with really wanted to be with *that* guy. Oh, they wouldn't admit it, but it was apparent when *that* guy was around. The flirtation, laughing, and attention was given so freely, almost as if they couldn't help themselves. The comments and suggestions were subtle but always came back to make him more like *that* guy.

"He did deal with his fair share of ladies who liked him for him but would never be seen in public with him. It would have been a scandal. In the end, he was never enough of one thing and was too much of another. He could be a great friend, or maybe just a good friend, but not a boyfriend.

"As my Leo got older, he grew into all sorts of man-things but never shook that feeling of not being enough. I may not have told him or showed him as often as he would have liked. Yet, Leo understood that those needs weren't as real as they felt. That I loved him and thought very highly of him. It got worse as his memory faded because he needed reminding more often. Otherwise, he'd get trapped in this cycle of focusing on what he perceived as flaws. All in some misguided effort to please me."

Donna interrupts, "You know, Julia. I never realized others could have mistreated a nice guy like him."

"It's funny," Julia replies. "He always said that it wasn't their fault. He said their parents made them that way, but he hoped they would learn over time. He hoped that they wouldn't teach their kids the same ways.

"Leo always had a belief that he was apprehensive about sharing. This drove him in many ways. You see, he believed that one of mankind's responsibilities was to teach others through the sharing of their experiences. He would always use the example of those ancient Martial Arts Masters in popular culture. Apparently, they were said to never teach their students everything they knew. As though, keeping their best moves a secret ensured they couldn't be conquered by a 'true master'--his words. Leo said, 'Like them, sharing with others our life experience was to afford them the chance to learn from our mistakes as well as our successes.'

"There was a quote," Julia continues, "that he liked. He wasn't sure of the use of the word 'power,' but otherwise, he said it was important for people to understand their egos always got in the way."

After a very brief moment of silence to remember what Leo said, Julia recalls, "Oh yeah. It was a quote from Bill Gates. *'Power comes not from knowledge kept but from knowledge shared.'*

"Leo would tell me that everything we learn we take with us to the 'Great Link,' but that is a conversation for another day. Sadly, his illness made simple conversations challenging. Given his skill at writing, this is why I encouraged him to write short stories."

"I think it might be time to read some of his writings." Donna suggests.

Julia replies, "What do you mean? Oh, right, the box. Donna, answer me honestly. Have you read them already?"

"Absolutely not. Leo was very clear that you were the only one to read them." Donna leans over and gives Julia a big hug before gathering her things.

Julia realizes Donna is leaving and gets up to walk her out. "Donna, I can't thank you enough for stopping by. I guess I have a lot to think about."

Donna starts laughing as she presses the fob for her car. Turning to Julia, she says, "You mean to say you have a lot of reflecting to do?"

Julia is stunned for a moment before she says, "That son of a ... 'Reflection'--he did it again."

LOVE MAGIC

Before leaving, Donna pulls a letter from her purse. She hands Julia the envelope and says, "I'm told this contains instructions, but I'm going to assume he'll have more to say. If you need me, I can video chat with you while you read it. No questions asked." Donna pauses for a moment, "Dammit, speaking of video chat, that reminds me. Hang on."

Donna runs to her car and comes back carrying a box. She gives Julia a package and says, "You are so lucky. Had I paid more attention, I might have tried to steal him. Here is that new video chat device. He made me promise I'd set one up and bring you one. Leo said you like to be alone but knew you'd need an effortless way to keep people in your life, and it was now my duty to be there. But, honey, I think I've danced on your emotions enough for one night. I'm going to go home and 'reflect' on David." Using air quotes and a smile, Donna hugs Julia, and Julia walks her to the door.

"Thank you, Donna. I can't thank you enough for stopping by. Goodnight," she says.

After watching Donna drive off, Julia goes back to the couch, where Leo's box sits, and places the new video device next to it.

Julia giggles, remembering when Leo wanted to keep her company using her cellphone's video call app since he couldn't accompany her like he used to. Leo meant well, but he tested her limits without a doubt. Julia loved him dearly.

Leo would have felt so guilty if Julia told him how it made her feel. There were times when it made her feel like he didn't think she was capable of going about her day alone.

Even worse, sometimes, she felt like he didn't trust her. As though he needed to be there and monitor things. He didn't feel that way, but intent or lack thereof, doesn't remove hurt.

He would have blamed himself. Julia often tried to spare Leo from her feelings, especially as he got worse. She feared telling him would start a cycle of Leo analyzing his version of chivalry.

She knew that he would only be reminded that he caused her to hurt and blame himself despite his lack of control over the entire thing. Telling him when he made her feel that way was what folks like Leo have to struggle with. She wouldn't wish it on anyone, nor would she intentionally add to it.

Taking a deep breath, Julia decided to get a cup of tea and settle in bed before reading the letter. She couldn't think of a better place to say hi to her Leo.

For her and Leo, bedtime was a cherished event. It was a sacred portion of their day observed in a safe and protective location.

Julia remembered when Leo said, "The bed is the center of one's marriage."

"Just like a guy to think that," Julia teased, knowing he had trouble getting his words out.

"No, not like that. I'll rephrase. The bed is the nexus of a healthy marriage. Does that sound better?" Leo replied.

Julia knew he wasn't implying the bed represented the sexual congress that might occur there, so she asked, "Okay, babe, I'll bite. Explain," Julia said.

"In every healthy marriage, the marital bed is where all the important things happen. Where things are discussed, sorted out--

the list just goes on. When you want to have kids, you lay in bed and discuss it before going to sleep. When there is trouble anywhere in the house--with the kids, work, money, family ....
When a partner is sick--the bed exercises its gravity once again. In a healthy relationship, the bed permeates all areas of your life.

"When things are good, everything circles back to the bed. From the little kiss that greets your love in the morning to the exhausted body that drifts off to sleep at night, the bed serves the marriage. I think so, anyway."

Julia responded by telling Leo, "And that's why I married you, sweetie."

"Why," Leo asked, "because I'm handsome and brilliant?

She giggled with a smile on her face. Julia said, "You got me, baby. Sure. That, and because you think of such things."

This memory brings a new giggle to Julia. She hears it and realizes, until today with Donna, it has been a long while since she last giggled. Before today, she honestly wasn't sure she could again, but thankfully, Leo had seen it in advance. Though, she never cared for the self-deprecating comments.

It was a notion Leo despised. Not specifically those doing it, like himself, but rather whoever started this practice or engineered what Leo considered a design flaw.

Changing into her nightclothes, Julia wears Leo's favorite ensemble. He was a randy fellow right up until the end. His favorite was not some frilly fancy lingerie.

Leo's favorite outfit to see Julia come to bed in was an old t-shirt and her comfortable cotton panties. Julia loved that about him. It was nice knowing that her most comfortable outfit was his favorite.

Though, once she asked him why because she wasn't sure.

Leo replied, "When you are comfortable, your energy is so much brighter. That turns me on more than any lace or silk get-up. You being you is my thing. Keep doing that."

She'd often wonder if it was some kind of trick, but in the end, Leo meant what he said. He wanted very much to be the smooth operator he felt Julia deserved, and though it was often a failure-- there was no doubt he meant all the corny mushy words he'd fail to deliver successfully.

Speaking of which, Julia thinks, *what kooky thing is in this letter.*

With her tea by the bedside, she hops up in the middle and arranges the pillows just so. For ambiance, she puts on Leo's favorite movie, *Bicentennial Man.* Well, maybe not his favorite, but certainly in the top 10.

He watched it repeatedly.

Now in bed, Julia proceeds to open the letter. She isn't sure what to expect, but she's excited to read his words. She hopes Leo had written it on a good day. Those became fewer and fewer as the illness progressed.

Now thinking about it, Leo's smile was the one thing that never changed. Sure, it might not have been as available as things worsened, but it was the same as always when it occurred. Unchanged like a secret word to let you know it's really him. His smile; quirky in its uniqueness.

Bedtime was precisely the place Leo would showcase his smile. Whether they cuddled, became intimate, or just watched TV, Leo was always making jokes and smiling. He would not have succeeded as a stage comic, but he did manage to bring Julia smiles and laughter.

She never told him, but he could manage a smile out of her even when she was grumpy. A laugh could turn the day around. Leo made sure when they went to bed, they had something to watch. Something they both enjoyed. He'd say that Julia got so busy it was the only time they could do a little traveling together. New movies or series they could binge-watch. Leo said sharing a timeline from a show or movie helped to keep them tethered. She wasn't entirely sure what he'd meant, but no doubt it was a part of one of Leo's theories.

Those theories kept Leo sane for a long time. He would go on about them. It was the kind of thing they did in bed. Discussing all the things a busy day leaves little time for. Leo thought deep and hard. Their lives and her happiness were always at the center.

The further along the illness got, the less likely the night before mattered to his moods in his morning. The mental resets were becoming more and more real. He would treasure their time in the bed even more by staying up on good days. It wasn't healthy, but she understood, so she tried to balance his sleep out on bad days.

The envelope was addressed to 'Noodle,' Leo's nickname for her.

Julia's mother once commented during a stay early in their marriage, "Close your door. I don't wanna hear you canoodle."

Julia had the cutest reaction as she blushed in a way Leo had never witnessed before, and from that day forward, Leo called her his 'Noodle.' Julia protested initially, but it was a special memory for them, and she grew to love the nickname. Though, it later became a name he'd use when he needed her love and validation. Some days his sanity depended on it.

He'd say, "You only know what's true when you can trust what you know."

Ensuring the tissue box is nearby, Julia peels back the fold on the envelope. She slides out the letter inside. Julia can't remember being this nervous about reading a letter. For once in her dealings with Leo, she is on edge in her uncertainty of what to expect, like she is about to have an unpredictable conversation. Not to mention it has been some time since she's had a private conversation with her Leo.

She knows that once she unfolds the sheet of paper, Leo will be waiting for her. She will get to speak with him once again. Honestly, she isn't entirely sure she can handle it.

Without thinking, she grabs her cell phone and calls Donna.

"What took you so long?" is how Donna answers the phone. "Are you in bed yet?" Donna asks.

"How the hell could you know that?"

Donna replies, "I asked him once how he could be so confident in his predictions. Leo called it his Love Magic."

CHAPTER
ELEVEN

HELLO, NOODLE

"So in the bed yet?" Donna asks again, and Julia confirms. Donna continues, "Okay, put the phone on speaker and set it down next to you."

"Done."

"Now, open the letter slowly and read it out loud."

Unfurling the paper, Julia notices an aroma. "What's the smell? Is that?" Julia asks.

"What? What smell?"

It takes Julia a minute, then she says, "That's my Leo's cologne. Oh, that man knows me." Julia loves the scent. She never let Leo run out, and he knew it. He would enjoy a fresh application when he was in the mood.

"What else?" Donna asks eagerly.

Julia tells her to calm down; she is about to start reading.

My Dearest Julia,

I see you. Please don't cry.

Just breathe slow, deep breaths, and read carefully.

I cannot fathom what you are feeling, going through, dealing with, and all around have to bounce around inside your head.

If you're reading this, you've received a visit from Donna. Don't be mad at me. Allow me to explain.

You see, earlier today, Buttercup stopped by, and we had cereal. You know how we do.

Anyway, we got to talking about you, how we met, and generally just her listening to me tell my overstated love tale. Just the way I like to.

As I danced with my thoughts of you, I reveled amidst all the joyous memories, and I realized what was to come, and I felt fear. Not fear for me. Fear for you.

I was suddenly fearful, though as I realized with me, you're used to everything old also being new again. Yet, I couldn't help but feel like I forgot to do something. Something for you.

The time with Buttercup made me realize what I needed to do. I needed to ensure I was there to help. I wanted to find a way to be by your side in your time of grief, sorrow, and profound change. In all our years together, I can't think of a time you will need me more. Somehow. Some way.

To this end, I decided the best thing I could do was arrange a few surprises. Just like the good ole days, am I right?

You know what I mean.

Back when walking, talking, and thinking was still in my wheel-

house, I remember all the goofball grand gestures I orchestrated simply to elicit a smile. I'd had all sorts of mostly juvenile ideas.

Just like the time I proposed simply because it was our anniversary, or the public spectacle I made doing it at your work, I am going to express my love upon you for the final time.

This time I cannot do it in person, so I've lined up a few surrogates. Donna, of course, has already shown up. She will be pivotal to my plan—details to follow. Of course, my little Buttercup will make a few appearances. Don't be too hard on her.

Let me be unambiguous, my queen. You don't need my help and maybe don't want it. That's okay. You are a strong independent woman. You know I have never strived to be a man who thinks you can't get on without me. After all, you spent most of our lives taking care of me.

The purpose of this is not to suggest in any way, shape, or form that you can't get on without me but rather to show you that you absolutely can when most people doubt themselves the most. To be honest, I would kind of prefer you did. Here's why.

Now, this may surprise you, or not, but I have secretly spent my life as an outsider. Even when I was barely learning to read, I became exceedingly curious. Mostly about people but also how the world worked. These kinds of thoughts led to interests that somehow set me apart from others and not in the best way. I grew up around a lot of people, knew a lot of people, and would even be recognized and greeted by far more people than I can remember anymore, but I've never really been diehard friends with any of them.

I'm sure I've never really heard from anyone as an adult who wasn't going through something in their lives and needed some-

thing from me. Ultimately, I'd advise them best I could and always knew when this moment had passed. It was easy. That's when I wouldn't hear much from them—eventually resulting in just not hearing from them anymore.

Over time, I have become comfortable in that role. I've learned a great deal and met a great many different kinds of people. I've helped where I could and apologized for my mistakes where I could. I've learned from everything that's ever happened to me and found joy in doing for others when I could.

But most of all, my love, I was blessed with your love and presence.

Before meeting you, I was in a relationship that felt very much like more of the same outsider roles I'd filled. You taught me what it was to be the center of someone's attention.

Despite the lack of my machismo mindset, you managed to make me feel like 'that guy.' That celeb the women go crazy for—the Rock Star who gets marriage proposals daily. And yes, even the adult film star who puts on a quality performance. And yes, is it entirely shallow and self-centered? Absolutely.

Though, I would argue that every one of us has a place where this feeling just fuels us for success, it's a small measure of energy rejuvenation. It feeds our confidence and self-image. As a society, we preach against this as a life goal, and for many good reasons, selfishness is wrong.

The thing is when this feeling is offered to you because someone else makes you want to feel that way, that is nothing short of a gift—a gift of indescribable value.

For this, I can never thank you enough. You have also taught me what it is to be someone I am not. Someone like you.

You taught me that someone strong and beautiful could also be fragile and shy. I've seen you walk into a room and draw all the attention. The thing is, the focus was never aimed in any particular direction. Your collective traits--brain, beauty, strength, independence, dependability, natural leader, and confidence shine in a way that many aren't used to.

Everyone always had compliments and usually needed help with something but often just a question. Sometimes it was as though their professor had entered the room. A marvel to behold.

I have seen you help all those who cross your path and devote your life to our children and family. In the midst of that, I have seen you continue your education--always setting the example that life is no excuse to stop bettering yourself. A role model every child should have. Our children are luckier than they can probably understand adequately for some time yet.

My research suggests to me that when one loses a spouse, there are all kinds of things one misses. Yet, the one that stands out most to me is the inability to have conversations. The ones about your day. The daily occurrences that we share with our mates.

In most cases, it's the simple milestones of life that we share with our loved ones. We both know no marriage can survive without discourse, and discourse is the second most intimate sharing activity a couple can practice.

What's important to remember is that inside this box is an assortment of letters and stories. They embrace a wide range of topics and memories.

Some are meant to allow us to reminisce while others are my way of being there with advice, opinions, and the general two cents I would offer around the house.

I thought to myself, how can I help? When you get home from work, there are a few letters that will facilitate a conversation of sorts. When you are bored or just want to talk, I've provided a few stories that should help get that conversation going.

I know I'm not there, but is that a reason for us not to talk? Even if the memory of it is only in your head, it still happened. Surprisingly, there is a lot that a human brain can get from such a conversation.

It is my hope that the writings will provide a bridge to help you get from a place of longing and mourning to a place of happy memories and a desire to make new ones.

Now tucked in the bottom of the box is a more intimate letter for you. I'd say, 'Please don't share with Donna,' but let's be honest here. It doesn't matter if you share; I am now a part of your past. Share and dwell, but enjoy the memories. Let's call it a bit of a companion letter because, like it or not, that may require some adjustment.

I hope after you read it all, you'll find the transition to your new chapter less painful. Perhaps after you've read your favorites a few times, they will all end up back in this box as remnants of a beautiful past with memories you'll return to often but not too often.

Maybe you'll get them out once in a while, but it is most vital that you get on with life. I have witnessed what happens when life just slips away while you are besieged by negativity. I do not want this to happen to you.

We will take a little journey, and when it's over, I hope you will smile at the thought of me yet be fully invested with the 2nd chance at life around you.

I want to convince you to make it your best go yet. With whatever passes for a smile on this side of the rim, I remind you of the quote you borrowed from one of my favorite role models.

This is probably not what you were expecting me to say, but here is why I feel it's the best thing to tell you.

I can go on and on with riveting detail about how much I love and how much I miss you. There are so many apparent ways for me to communicate what you represent to me. Just all the lovely, mushy, kissy kissy, googly stuff that didn't always win you over.

You also showed me that anytime I was an idiot, you might have gotten upset as you were undoubtedly entitled to, but it didn't change what you did. You cared for me, cleaned after me, and made sure I didn't starve to death.

You cooked foods that you knew would put a smile on my face. Even when no one else wanted what I did, you still made me a portion. I never had to ask for things; they just showed up.

The cleanliness of my life shouldn't go without saying. You did so much more than you'll ever get proper credit for.

Most importantly, you never let me forget those little words. So today, I will return them to you.

I apologize from the depths of my soul for all the heartache and betrayal I brought to your life, albeit unintentionally. Despite all the joy I extracted from your life, you always found the time to bring some joy to mine. It was one-sided and unfair in so many ways. Just having you in my life added years to it. Thank you.

"However bad life may seem, there is always something you can do and succeed at. Where there's life, there's hope." — Stephen Hawking

I love you. I love you in ways I never knew were possible. At least not until you showed me, taught me, and explored with me. You showed me emotions. I discovered those things on my journey with you and am thankful.

Not to put too fine a point on it, but--I am not there anymore. I'm not coming back, at least not how you'd imagine. I know it's brutal, but there it is. Maybe I will blow the curtains around or knock something off your desk. Perhaps not, but we shall see as I learn my way around this new place.

In the meantime, your time on Earth has not reached its conclusion. Therefore, I am going to need you to call Donna and ask her to take you out. Nothing crazy at first.

Now, Donna has instructions and a sort of schedule on when to call you and what to invite you to should you try to brush her off and concede to isolation. Neither she nor I will allow that attitude to grow, so prepare yourself now. Small outings--dinner, movies, and maybe a craft fair. Things I know you enjoy, starting with the less crowded ones first.

I understand your apprehension, which is why she will have more letters for you as you go. I've timed it out to last no more than the first year. I will be with you in my words for any number of occasions and events. Donna will have a letter on certain occasions.

To avoid you asking Donna for them all right away, just note that

Donna doesn't have the letters. She, too, will get them when they are needed.

For the time being, I have filled this box with several of my writings. They are meant to allow us conversations beyond what is possible. It may be like when I used to read you stories. Instead, now you read mine.

Before I end this letter, I want to ask you one thing. Do not let my death hold you back. I spent far too many of my living years holding you back from friends, life, and living. All the arguments over your sacrifices can't change that the time is gone.

I encourage you to embrace the world once again. Enjoy life the way you once taught me.

May the next leg of your journey bring you all the joy you brought to my life.

Your devoted husband, best friend, lover, and life partner,

Eternally, Leo

SUDDENLY, the room falls silent. Not even her tears break the quiet. Her mind is frozen in time as she attempts to process her Leo's words. She misses him so much, but for this brief moment, it was as though he was there with her.

Julia's grip tightens on the letter, trying to stop her shaking hands. It's a physical reaction to the overwhelming emotions she is feeling. One for which no words will truly do justice. Like the moment one hold their baby for the first time. You have thought about it over and over t hose 9-10 months but finding yourself in that moment leaves you speechless.

Eventually, she wonders, 'What is she even to make of this?'

"Oh my God!" Donna breaks the silence with her squeals. "Oh my God! Oh my God! Julia, are you okay?" Donna pauses, and comes back more gentle as Julia's silence continues. "Honey, do you want me to come back over?"

The cloud of silence extends.

Donna repeats, "Julia, are you oka..."

Julia interrupts, "P.S. Text James. It's in my contacts under 'The Order.'"

Donna yells out, "Who the hell is James?' And what's 'The Order?'"

Julia blinks a few times, her brows narrowing. "Those are two excellent questions!"

CHAPTER
TWELVE

THE HUNT CONTINUES

"Are you sure you don't want me to come by?" Donna asks.

"No, really, it's okay. I'm just going to drink some tea and turn in. It's been an emotional day, and I'd like to just turn my brain off. I trust you know what I mean," Julia replies.

Good-byes are exchanged, and Julia reaches for her tea on the bedside table.

James … who's James … I don't remember any James. The thoughts roll through her head in a flurry.

It occurs to her that there was only one thing in his life with 'Order' in the title--his gaming guilds. She might have told Donna she was heading to bed. She might even have had every intention of heading to bed, but now the only thing Julia can think about is James and the Order.

Putting down her tea, Julia goes straight to Leo's den. Slowly, she opens the door. Julia has not been in here since Leo left for the rim.

It still smells like him. It's funny how subtle aromas can exist unnoticed until a memory is triggered.

For Julia, memories are all she has left, or so she thought.

Approaching his desk, Julia feels hesitant. She doesn't want to disrupt anything. Caught in a moment, she feels like he'd be annoyed by someone moving things on his desk. He wasn't possessive about it, but Leo depended on knowing where all his stuff was. Moving things on his desk was akin to moving the furniture on a blind person. His mind had to work harder when things weren't always in the same place.

Still, she has to remind herself that the issue is now moot. Nothing she does now will affect him. She hopes that he's found some peace.

Okay, James, where did he put that number?

Turning on his computer, Julia wonders what his password is. *Never mind*, she thinks, *I know precisely what it is.* Leo was nothing if not predictable.

On the other hand, the computer, as much as the world loves and invests in technology, always proves it can still be inconvenient. Case in point, when the computer boots up, it decides now is the perfect time for an update. Sure, her internal screaming is reaching a new high, but what could she do?

Vent! That's what.

Grabbing her cellphone, Julia dials Donna and is met with a sarcastic, "Couldn't sleep, huh?"

"You just shut your mouth. Now tell me who this James could be."

Of course, Donna asks, "Did you look in his computer?"

"Yes, Donna, but the computer decided its update time. So, any ideas?" Julia sighs.

All Donna can do is try and comfort her. "Oh, honey, I shouldn't have left you. Take a deep breath while the machine works, and let's think. Was he a part of any community groups that maybe you didn't attend?"

Running through the options leaves them empty-handed. Since moving to The Mountain, his contact with others was closely monitored for his safety and security.

"I'll have to call Natalie. She manages the visitors at The

Mountain; maybe she knows something. What time is it?" Julia asks.

"Let's see. My phone says 7:25 p.m."

Julia says, "Okay, then I can--"

"No, wait," Donna interrupts. "I forgot to grab my glasses. It says 8:25 p.m."

"Really, Donna, do you still have issues wearing those glasses?"

"Well, they make me look old."

"Fine," Julia begins, "and how do you think not being able to see makes you look?" She's met with silence. "We'll come back to this later, but can't you just get a different pair? Wait, the computer is back."

WATCHING THE COMPUTER STARTUP, Julia is struck with deep emotions as she sees the pictures that are now revealed. Leo's themes always included his favorite photos of Julia. He also had little post-it's on his computer, that digital kind that followed him across his devices. He found it was the best way to remind himself of things in the early days.

Amongst all the reminders were things others wouldn't expect.

Leo had laid out all his stickies in groups separated by color. They broke things down into categories like kids, games, house stuff, pets, and so on. Inside each of those groups was a random reminder regarding Julia.

One says, "Stop what you are doing and go hug Julia, kiss her cheek, and thank her for all she does for you." Ugh, Julia had forgotten the lengths he went to. He had often worried that one day he would stop doing the things a husband should do.

Among them was his belief that irrespective of actions, one should always verbally and physically express your love, emotion, and yes, the attraction for one another. He said he learned that humans aren't built to go long-term without those reminders, especially after he stayed home with the kids for long periods of time.

Leo said we cut out too many things in relationships because we assume they just know. That is what he believed led couples to lose a certain closeness over time unless they make an effort to hold on to it. He claimed that those who research these fields likely have data to support his belief. He argued that the amount of data on humans far exceeds that which society lives by.

Leo would say studies have long governed the entire work-force. Studies with regards to productivity levels with and without supervision, yet the studies on people and power haven't moved the needle on issues with immediate impact. Things like term limits or our approach to high-stress careers. Nothing about their effect both on the employee and the work.

Julia misses how he could go on about things no one ever seemed to understand or care about--well, some did, but many people didn't like talking about them.

"Julia, are you okay?" Donna asks.

"What? Oh yeah, just got distracted by his setup. Do you remember how he used to randomly come up to me while you and I were talking? Then he'd get mushy, and I'd shush him away?" Julia asks.

"Of course, I always felt kind of bad for him at that point," Donna says. "He'd look like he got scolded walking away. Though, now that I understand him better, I think it's fair to say he never really thought you were scolding him. I believe his looks and reactions were more because he had rudely interrupted. Again.

"In fact, I'm just remembering when talking to him last, he mentioned that one of the worst parts of this was him being rude to others. He felt that the illness was making him a person he didn't want to be. Different is one thing, but a person he wasn't fond of was a lot to deal with emotionally. I can't say I blame him. I'd hate to be forced to be someone I'm not. There couldn't have been anything that made it comfortable, especially over time. That had to be a compoundable ugly feeling, if I'm honest." Donna abruptly stops talking.

It's likely only been a few seconds, but it seems like minutes were just racking up before Julia says, "Donna."

"I'm here."

"I think you are correct. I think he was dealing with far more than even I had considered. As I look around his office, I can't help but notice all the subtle aspects of his life I didn't give much weight to before."

"Holy crap!" Donna exclaims.

"What?"

"He did it again. I can't believe it. Your Leo was some kind of … I don't know … wizard. Think about what you just said."

Julia thinks for a moment.

Donna declares, "He is laughing. I know it. Maybe just smiling, but whatever."

Julia is still thinking, *What is Donna talking about?*

Suddenly, Julia blurts out, "I love you, Leo, but that is not funny. Donna, I'm getting the impression that my Leo was there right up to the end. We just couldn't see him inside his machine. Honestly, though, do you think maybe I made him feel like that?"

"Here is what I think. I believe that whatever journey he hoped he could help with would not include anything meant to blame you or make you feel bad. For him, the past was past. Live and learn--just make sure you learn. Never forget, and he said to me, 'You can construct your future from the lessons of the past or let it unfold like moss on a tree.' I don't think I understood that until now." After a slight pause, "Crap, he got me again."

Now, they are both laughing. Julia sounds like she is going to pee herself any minute, but it has been too long since she last laughed this much.

Donna asks Julia as their laughter dies down, "Should we find this James?"

That is the snap Julia needs. There is a reason she is in his office. *Who is James? Why did Leo want her to contact him?*

． ． ．

Back on the mission, Julia starts to search.

Leo had grown cautious over time. Removing friends and family from his contacts and social media. He was worried his bad habits would surface by trying to communicate with them. It weighed on his mind that he might post something unfunny or, worse, inappropriate in social media settings or really anywhere. This lack of connection always worried Julia. Every person requires different types of contact and connection.

Unfortunately, for folks like her Leo, Julia knows that avenues to fulfill those human needs are challenging. This is one of the reasons why she encouraged him to play his online games. He could explore these made-up worlds from his chair. He could run, ride, fly, and in general, escape his everyday circumstances in a safe environment. Leo would comment on all the conversations in the public chat spaces used by all players, all while never having to engage in person with anyone.

Julia knew that while he found some peace and joy in playing his games, he would often avoid it out of guilt. Sure, he had nothing else productive he could accomplish on a particular day, but she'd watch him struggle to get into his game for feeling like he should be doing something else for the benefit of his family. It was often painful to watch. Julia tried to ease his burden through Loving Trickery.

Now 'Loving Trickery' is what he called her skill where she used her knowledge of Leo against him. Like, getting him to eat things he needed but didn't like. For example, Julia would ask him for help with something, just a small task that seemed neither complicated nor un-doable by Leo, and after Leo had done her the 'favor,' she'd say, 'Now that you've done some work today, why don't you play your games.' He'd then go off and play for a few hours without the guilt. Leo had said Julia had a Master's degree in Loving Trickery. He made her a faux diploma from the University of Love Magic.

Julia had thought it was cute, and ultimately, she knew that he was fully aware of her methods. He'd openly expressed his approval of her using such an approach. Julia had resisted at first as she was naturally a straight shooter, but eventually, she came around, and they both found wisdom and mercy in it.

HER THOUGHTS ARE ONCE AGAIN INTERRUPTED by her awesome yet annoying friend.

"Did you find it?" Donna hollers through the phone.

Julia searches for the word 'Order,' and there it is. James is listed as the only name associated with it. Just one phone number with a note, 'Text first.'

After relaying the discovery to Donna, Julia's friend urges her to get her bluetooth so she can free up her hands.

Moments later, the ladies are ready.

Julia tells Donna, "Okay, I'm hands-free and ready to call him."

Donna reminds her of the note to text first.

"Okay, Okay, here we go." Typing the phone number in, she asks Donna, "Wait. What should I type?"

Donna says, "Just put your name and explain you were told to contact a James."

Julia pauses before talking as she types, "Hello, my name is Julia. My husband, Leo, asked me to contact this number and ask for James. Is he available?" Then returning to Donna, she asks, "What do you think?"

"If you don't hit send, I'm going to come over there and text him myself."

Julia sighs, "Alright, alright .... and send."

Donna and Julia begin discussing what to do now and who James could be and are interrupted less than two minutes later by a chime.

As Julia checks her phone, Donna reminds her to read the text out loud.

Julia giggles. It is a reply from James, but had Donna not said it, she probably would have forgotten about her presence.

"Come on, what does it say? Is it from him? Hey, wait, it's kind of late. Is there someone I don't know about?"

Julia says, "You shut it. Not funny."

Julia understands Donna's humor, but now is not the time and place to joke about her having another partner.

Julia continues, "It is from the number and says, 'Hello Julia, I am James. I have been expecting your call. I am available at your convenience to explain who I am and why Leo would want you to call me. Please feel free to invite Donna as I'm sure she also has questions. Also, since we've never met, it would be more appropriate.

"Additionally, there is someone you do know who would love to say hello. Assuming you've spoken to Donna already, she would also get to do some catching up. Please let me know, and yes, now and tonight are okay. It's not far; perhaps Donna could drive if you don't yet feel up to it. Speak soon, James."

"Donna, what do I say? Do you think it's too late?" Julia asks.

Donna replies as only she could, "First, why am I involved in all this, and tell him I am on my way and we'd like to meet in 20 minutes. Given the time, it will have to be your house or his, but I'm not worried. Leo would never put you in a dangerous situation. Normally, I'd caution public places, but something tells me that husband of yours only wants to put a smile on your face. Okay, tell him that, and I'm on my way to get you."

Then she hangs up.

JULIA STARES at her phone for a moment feeling like it's all been a bit surreal. Just this morning, she was without any purpose to breathe. Now, she is in the middle of some kind of mystery.

Taking a moment, she just smiles to herself and thinks, *Thank you, baby.*

HIS SECRET LIFE

I 5 minutes later, Donna is knocking on the front door.

Julia feels strange. Can it be happy? Maybe excitement?

After letting her in, Donna hits Julia with all the questions. Julia explains that she wrote James back and that James said it'd have to be his house as he has children. Though now would work, and they are both welcome.

"James also said it would work for this 'friend' of ours as they live closer to him."

Not wanting to get into another discussion, Julia grabs her stuff and heads for the door. Donna follows behind.

As Julia is putting the address into Donna's GPS, Donna says, "I feel like I know that neighborhood. I just can't place it."

Julia doesn't recognize the address at all. Nor the area of town.

It's a beautiful area. The houses are not million-dollar mansions, but they appear to be both spacious and loaded with amenities. You can see some slides peeking out from a few backyards. They appear to be the type commonly associated with in-ground pools.

This is what some may call a comfortable country living.

Oddly enough, these properties aren't really in the country but are designed to make you feel that way. Leo used to go on about features like these. Urban settings with a country feel. Privacy and perspective can change the way people feel at home, he would contend.

One of his many interests for which he could never pursue was architecture and home design. For all the science and math involved, he thought that these homes never factored in human beings living there as much as making sure the design looked good. He believed it was an inflated industry that could be done better and cheaper without such a waste of natural resources.

He would say, "People get so wrapped up in individual issues that they lose sight of simply doing it better for less with less. We are capable of so much more than one can profit from. The loss to humanity and its evolution is probably incalculable. At some point, capitalism will have to find its limits if humanity is to move forward better instead of worse."

Leo tended to get passionate in his conversations about what he believed were the real issues society should talk about.

Julia thinks about what he'd say about this neighborhood, but as they get closer, she thinks he might like it. It's a gated community; James had given them the passcode to enter. He loved the idea of those. The area outside is lined with trees so that no one can see anything but the gate. As you enter, it's like its own little town. They even have a small gas station/grocery in the middle of it.

Driving through the community, Julia can't help but be slack-jawed by all the little design ideas that Leo would have loved. She even recognized some as ideas he'd previously discussed.

Donna speaks up. "This seems like the kind of neighborhood where people frequently talk to each other." She adds, "In my neighborhood, people barely recognize each other, never mind have more than 2-minute conversations."

Julia replies, "I know. Can't say I wouldn't mind living here myself."

Just then, the GPS talks. "Take the next right. Then you will have arrived at your destination. Hurry back, Donna."

"Really, Donna?" Julia asks, laughing. "And was that the sexiest voice you could find?"

"Hey, a girl has to be excited to get where she's going, or the day would just drag on. What do you want from me, Lucifer Morningstar's voice was on sale and we both know *the devil made me do it*?" Donna defends with a smile and leaves it at that.

Julia just shakes her head.

Coming around the corner, they both grow excited, but as they inch closer to parking, Julia exclaims, "Wait!"

Donna ignores her pleas. "Julia, maybe it's weird for me to say, but I trust Leo, so I'm going to force you to ring that bell. I am parking this car, and we are going to that door if I have to drag you. Besides, if I don't, Leo will probably find a way to haunt me."

Julia laughs as she starts getting out of the car.

It's no surprise that the front door opens just as they are getting out of the car. Donna isn't known for her soft touch or quiet mannerisms, case-in-point, she makes a lot of noise getting out of a car.

Julia is quite used to the attention and looks that come with Donna's noise. In this case, she looks up at the door and sees the figure of a young man standing on the front porch.

Neither of them recognizes the house right off. As they begin walking the relatively long sidewalk to the front door, Julia notices a shadow behind the young man, who she assumes is James.

Suddenly, the shadow is coming toward them, and just as the shadow passes through the porch lights, the voice speaks.

"Hey, girlies! I am so glad to see you both. Julia, I'm so, so sorry but incredibly happy you are here. Oh, and don't worry, there is nothing but good news waiting for you. Donna, you haven't changed a bit. Please come on inside. Meet my husband and take a load off. I have no doubt it has been an emotionally challenging day for you both. So let's get inside and get you some clarity. Shall we?"

This is intense. Standing before them is Josie, an old co-worker of both Julia and Donna. They had all become terrific friends with Josie, and they used to have lunch every day.

AT THE TIME, Josie was single, and Julia became like her big sister/mentor. In truth, Josie idolized Julia. She loved getting her advice and hearing about her experiences. Julia had lived the kind of life Josie wasn't aware she could.

Growing up, Josie had lived in a middle-class neighborhood with a nice house and safe streets. Her parents weren't ridiculously wealthy, but they had more than most. Her dad was a mid-level banker, and her mom was a high school teacher. In her youth, Josie was kind, friendly, and popular. In high school, she developed physically like most girls. But like most girls surrounding her, she was the chubby girl. No matter how hard she tried, she could never get to her ideal weight nor the love and attention she wanted.

Josie had an aunt who had a similar body type and unwittingly taught Josie that her body could get her the attention and, again, love. Love is what she truly wanted. Josie didn't realize that using her body to get attention was frowned upon, and her lifestyle was unwelcome by many women.

No matter how hard she watched her food and exercised, there was a roundness that wouldn't go away. Oh, how it infuriated her. The result was her finding other ways to become popular with the boys. Unfortunately, as Julia had to come to realize later--Josie's aunt had influenced the next stage of her high school experience.

It turned out her mother and her aunt grew up much like Julia did. A manly environment that didn't welcome change. Now while her mother was the perfect everything, her aunt was more like her physically. While she loved her aunt, many did not. They found her too provocative and forward with guests. You see, her aunt had found sex to be something that can easily result in attention and, by extension, love. Her willingness to share was not out of love for the sharing but rather a passion for the attention it brought. It made her feel loved.

Josie's aunt, Frankie, was not what society called a tramp by any stretch. Best Josie could remember she'd always had a few man friends in her life, but she didn't ask questions.

Sadly because there are so many topics hidden from children, Josie was never able to learn that her aunt never used her body the way Josie believed. Frankie was strong, independent, and Josie later learned, never relied on a man in life.

Most of these ideas she got from her mother. She was always pushing the end goal of kids and a man to take care of her.

Sadly that was part of why she was rarely around. Women like her aunt often found they were not welcome around most traditional relationships. Or they would say they understand and continually ask her about kids and marriage.

Julia and Josie grew closer as they often talked about the pressures placed on young women, particularly when a woman's life didn't go according to 'the plan.' Julia never once judged or condemned Josie but put in perspective the choices Josie was making and why they led to, of all things, a period of reflection for Josie.

Their conversations over time had not been overly revealing to Julia but showed a changing realization of what she was looking for in a relationship. Indeed, Josie was pursuing one now instead of waiting for it to show up at her door one day.

Julia remembered these stories as a prelude to a time when Josie had brought up a dilemma that she had found two of what she called 'perfect matches.' Josie was torn between the two men.

Enough so that they were the topic for a few days straight. During those few days, Julia had lots of questions. In the end, she suggested--if it were her--the first guy.

Julia's reasons were simple.

Guy number one, she called 'J.'

Josie had known him her whole life, and the sex was adequate. It was not dull. He inspired an energized environment. He had some quirks, but what man doesn't. And the biggest win of all was J secretly loved her in high school and hadn't liked what people said about her.

Josie had said that they always were talking; there was never a dull moment between the two. She said he'd take her to foreign films, and they'd occasionally go dancing at her favorite fancy restaurant.

Guy number two, she referred to as 'R,' and " had everything". Josie said he's gorgeous, and the sex was mind-blowing. Though, Josie soon came to realize that R's interests directly revolved around sex. And while it was easy to fall back on that, it wasn't the lifestyle Josie wanted.

Therefore, her decision was made; Josie had decided to break off contact with R and focus her attention on J.

J turned out to be James.

When Julia and Donna are on the porch, Josie says, "Julia, Donna--I would like to introduce you to my husband, James. Honey, this is my friend Donna."

Donna puts out her hand, and James takes her hand gently but firmly.

Josie continues, "And this is, of course, Julia. You know, she picked you. You owe her your life." Kissing her husband, Josie giggles while James steps forward toward Julia. He raises his arms open, but Julia hesitates as she looks him over.

He appears to be your average caucasian professional-looking male; dirty blonde hair and blue eyes. Not too tall or short. Not too thick or thin. He seems in shape, but she doesn't take him for an athlete. There is nothing about him that she can latch on to just yet--some understanding of what he had to do with her Leo and his secret life.

Her attention back in the present, Julia is unsure of his gesture until he says, "Would it be okay if I hugged you? I realize you don't even know me, but he made me swear I would the moment I came face to face with you. I'd rather not risk his otherworldly wrath."

Whether it was his words or smile, Julia could picture the empty threats her Leo had made. Like Donna, it was just a part of the memory her Leo left on these two people. Who is she to mess that up? She is just glad she isn't alone in loving and remembering him.

Opening her arms for James, she welcomes his bear hug.

James then whispers in her ear, "Can I give you his message?" Feeling Julia nod her head, James says, "This hug is from me. I will always be with you, no matter where you go. Now I am with you as support in whatever decisions you make going forward. Please don't ever make me the reason you are stuck in the past. I love you."

CHAPTER
FOURTEEN

INNOCENCE LOST

Julia starts crying at James' message from Leo, crying like she hasn't done all day.

In that split moment, Josie quickly moves in and switches places with James.

"Let it out," she whispers. Josie comforts James with, "It's okay, honey, we anticipated this. She'll be okay."

Donna catches on and takes James into his home while Josie stays outside a few minutes, holding Julia.

After a few minutes, Julia stops crying and starts to offer an apology.

Josie says, "Darling, there is nothing to apologize for. If anything, I should apologize to you. I feel like I've been lying or keeping secrets. We hardly ever see each other since I left that job, but we have so much to catch up on.

"In the meantime, what I will say is that Leo changed my life in more ways than I can count. Now, while you have always told me nothing is ever as perfect as it may seem from the outside, his advice to James has changed the life I might not have had without it. I'll let James get into the details. For now, know if you want to cry, then do it. Whatever you want, we are here for you. Truly anything."

With one final squeeze, Josie then takes Julia's hand and leads her into the house. Inside, Donna and James are at the island counter in the kitchen. Julia joins them while Josie walks off.

"Are you okay?" James asks.

"Yes, thank you," Julia replies.

"Leo said I might make you cry. He told Josie she'd have to be ready," James says. "That guy could be eerily accurate when you least expected it."

Entering the kitchen, Josie hands James a big folder. "Here, babe. You'll need this," Josie says while giving James a little peck. Then she takes some drink orders and goes about her business, but not before saying, "Don't forget the little ones are sleeping. Donna, that means you."

Donna did have a habit of waking sleeping children. She was viewed as the fun aunt, though lately, she has been less enthusiastic. Perhaps she is finally maturing.

Meanwhile, James is fidgeting with the folder.

"Julia, may I call you that? I feel like I already know you," James asks, and Julia nods. "Donna, I know about Leo's favor and am presuming that is how we got here. I'm also assuming," he looks over at Julia, "you have the small box he left with Donna. To that end, here is a key for a different larger box."

Julia and, of course, Donna are now entranced with what is to come. They share looks of wonder and slight confusion back and forth as they listen.

James adds, "The letter he left with Donna, I understand, is part of his little plan for you if you follow it. This chest I'm talking about is everything else. There are letters, stories, and writings of all kinds. He wanted you to have it all, but of course, I'm glad to hold on to what you don't take for as long as you need. I know he left a lot of writing to get through. Having exchanged correspondence with Leo, I know he's both deep and wordy. Sometimes I would have to wait a few days before reading one of his letters."

Julia asks, "Letters?"

"Yes, letters. Right, okay, see Leo and I were pen pals of a sort. You know what, let me backup to the beginning. I'll tell you how Leo and I connected, and the coincidence of Josie and you. All these connections that you weren't aware of, just know that he didn't want to keep secrets. In the beginning, it was just a few emails, and then it turned into something else. Much of it without his even knowing.

"That's when Leo decided to put this together. He wanted you to know this part of him in a way he could never communicate it. He hoped that knowing all this might help you move forward. Granted, I changed some of what we started, but I'll get to that. I know it's a lot of information to process. Let's get more comfortable."

They all move to the den, where Josie meets them with drinks before Julia and Donna turn their attention to James.

Julia and Donna are on the edge of their seats as they wait for James to continue.

"James, have you ever heard the adage 'Never Leave a Lady Waiting,'" Donna asks.

James gave a gentle smile, slight amusement in his eyes. "Not sure I have Donna, but what do you say we get to the story?"

Julia chimes in with, "Yes, please, James, I'm beyond ready."

James replies, "Of course, Julia. My apologies. I don't imagine there is anything else you want to talk about right now. Well, I suppose the beginning is the best place. To provide proper context, allow me to begin by telling you a pivotal moment in my own journey when my eyes were first opened. The object of this lesson was my mother."

•   •   •

Laying out the whole story, he discusses his relationship with his mother—and his dad's bad choices before his departure.

His mom had been without companionship for many years. Since entering high school with his male role model's guidance, he began to experience girls and relationships in a whole new way.

It led him to think that maybe he should encourage his mom to date again. He did love his mother and wanted her to be happy. You know, he wanted her to feel cared for and treated nicely, like he did his girlfriends.

In the beginning, it wasn't so bad.

He'd met two of the guys his mother had liked. Both had taken her to dinner and brought her home. Neither went anywhere past that.

The first guy turned out to be 'separated' from his wife, only to return to her shortly after that. He was friendly but clearly hadn't sorted out his old life before trying to start a new one.

The second guy ended up not calling his mother back after the dinner date.

When he had asked about it, she'd say, "it's okay he wasn't my type."

James had said, "He seemed cool. I thought he liked you." James remembers those compliments flowing. In hindsight, he realized the guy laid it on thick."

"Oh, honey, were you jealous?" His mother asked him.

He told her, "Mom, stop. It just rubbed me wrong. I'm not sure why. I figured he was just skilled with the ladies. You seemed happy."

"James, honey, don't you worry about me. I'll be okay. Maybe I should give him a call." His mom said.

Now, James was okay with this guy dating his mom. He didn't want to meddle in his mom's life, but he did want her to be happy.

The moment of reckoning for James came the Valentine's Day just before he reconnected with his now-wife, Josie.

His mom had been on a few more dates with the second guy, Georgie. It was coming up on the big "V" day, and James asked his mom if she had any plans.

His mother informed him, "Georgie said he was taking me to a fancy brunch at the country club. You can fend for yourself if I'm not back by dinner, right?"

Of course, he could, but his mother worried, "Yeah, mom, I'll be fine. Have fun." James then explained how he figured since he'd had nothing planned, he decided to hit one of his favorite spots for picking up women who'd been dumped. Since it was a jerk's favorite holiday to break up with a girl or was it the second. In any case, he was going to see what he could get into.

Humiliatingly, James admits he was basically on a hunt. He knew he had the house to himself, and he planned on doing something with that window of freedom. So off he went.

When he got there, he zoned in on his prey. In short order, they headed back to his house. The house all to himself, he was drowning in the things he wanted to do. Only making small talk with his companion, she had clearly outlined her willingness to get back at the two-timing coward who is now her ex.

Trying to be stealthy and sneak his guest in through the garage, he missed the car parked on the side street.

When they got inside, he heard voices and tried to shoo his guest back out. Whispering to her, James said, "We'll go some-where else. I have a spot."

That spot was his friend's apartment. His friend let him go there in tight spots because he had gotten promoted at work and kicked out his annoying roommate. James just didn't like making it a habit. Due in significant part to his friend getting the idea, he wanted to be the new roommate. Perhaps 'friends' wasn't an accurate description, but who is going to admit it.

As he ushered his guest back out quietly, James heard his mom say, "Stop."

It wasn't deafening, but his ears perked up. Now James didn't want to be nosey, but he certainly wasn't going to dismiss the notion his mom could be in trouble.

Giving his guest the key, he snuck back toward the family room. He could hear the conversation more clearly. His mom was okay, but they were arguing.

It sounded like the argument was because his mom kept saying, "No," "Because I just don't feel like it."

Then James heard it.

"I can't believe I spent all that money on you, and I don't get anything out of it."

THAT STATEMENT JAMES would find wrong in so many ways. It was one that highlighted, just brightly enough, the kind of ideas his male influences had and how much he didn't want to sound like that to other people.

He used to make the argument that he couldn't be held responsible for the feelings of others. He said he was always honest and upfront. He never sugar-coated anything or made promises he didn't keep. In truth, it was best just not to make any promises at all. Problem solved, right?

In--Out. Everyone gets what they want, knowing full well what they were in for. One could argue that this should be enough for any grown adult.

All grown adults can make their own choices. The problem is this application is being made by and amongst children.

Sure, the ripe old age of 18 is considered grown, but it also isn't.

On some level, advice requires context and foundation. The notions that kids get from parents, uncles, aunts, and the other older adults in their lives are given without those things. Like some ancient gurus, they hand out words failing to consider how their words translate across generations thoroughly.

In James' experience, most advice dispensed in such relationships is done in times of emotional turmoil. In others, the information is handed out expeditiously. It is done to satisfy an appropriate perceived responsibility or obligation, as opposed to taking the time from their busy lives to provide a well-considered response. This is not judgment but an observation.

"But what do I know, I was just a kid, right?" James said.

Through their conversations, Leo explained how he found adults who use the 'hard way' method both irresponsible and destructive.

Leo would tell me, "One cannot expect the young to simple absorb what you really meant when you handed out the advice. Sure, humans can easily remember and imprint on small phrases to remember lessons but the lessons themselves must be full, thoroughly explained and if at possible tested."

James explained how Leo would say, "Sadly this is rarely the case when it comes to advice given about relationships and connecting with other people."

Leo felt that their parents before them, living the mistakes does nothing to better educate our children. He felt that it only served to reaffirm bad habits and solidify behaviors and understanding before they are old enough to really form their own.

James was learning this to be the case for him as well. His behavior up until now would have made Georgie proud.

It was only after that fateful experience that James began realizing he didn't want to be anything like Georgie.

He could not make peace with hearing his mother cry.

James explained, "The one thing I came to realize is that what I wanted was what I had avoided for years. I wanted to be with one person all the time. Sure, I enjoyed years of partying and hanging out. The difference is that there is no future in it.

"When you get sick, no one is there. When you want to talk, you have to find someone who isn't busy. When you need help with something, it's the beginning of another search. It seems clear to me now that relationships are all about choosing that one person to be with all the time. One person, who also chooses you and with whom you can always count on in turn giving them the same."

BACK IN 15

J ames continuing with his story. He said, "I told you, Josie and I reconnected after that night. What I didn't tell you was 'How'"

"You see, after I here what was going on with my mom," James explained, "I walk in on them."

James said, "When I walked in, Georgie's eyes went big when I told him 'For the record your name is George. Georgie makes you sound like an idiot. Beat it idiot."

"I wasn't a big guy by any stretch, but I was certainly angry and he knew it. Thankfully Georgie just walked out. Though in those split seconds I became less concerned with the idiot and more concerned with my mother." James said.

James explained that he had inadvertently been pulled away from his anger by his deep sadness for his mom. Watching her cry James quickly put his arms around her trying to console her but was unsure how. All the while James was plagued with guilt for being anything like that guy.

"Once my mom had calmed down I told her 'I have to drop a friend off but I'll be right back. Is that okay?' and my mother responded, "of course sweetie go be with your friends," James said.

James recounted how on his way out he promised his mother 'I'll be back in 15 minutes. 18 tops.'

A promise.

He had made a honest to goodness promise.

This was new for James.

GETTING in the car he told his new friend, "I'm going to drop you off at the party. Something has come up." She seemed disappointed but readied herself for another round of partying.

On the way back to the party, James began to wonder about his friend.

He thought to himself, *Why was she with him? What happened to her that she ended up here in this situation?*

A place he was quickly realizing didn't make him happy. At least not in any way that he was used to.

Now on his way home he was flagged down by a neighbor. She lived on the street behind him. He had agreed to take her home. It was on his way.

James explained to Julia that after he got home there was a discussion. He and his mom talked about everything. She gave him a long overdue 'birds and the bees' conversation, or so she thought. She explained her position and how it led to the earlier events.

He in turn explained to her all the things he thought he knew. The guidance he's lived his love life by and what he hoped to gain from a relationship. According to James it was the kind of talk every parent should have with their kids.

Not those vague uninformative ones you get early on. Once they get to a certain age the conversation should be revisited.

They might think they know everything but ultimately, they are low level toons in a video game trying to survive in zones they have no business being in.

They are just not ready.

Now several days later James explains he ran into that same neighbor to whom he gave a ride home.

He said they'd been pretty good friend preadolescence. They played together as kids. Sometimes with a larger group and some-time by themselves.

James said, "Her Aunt was friendly with my mom." He explained that he and his neighbor weren't all that alike but apparently they had gone to school together.

James said they had even spent a summer where they were inseparable as kids.

"As we got older we drifted apart, each with our own lives and issues," James explained.

That ride had been the first time he'd interacted with his neighbor in several years.

As James tells it, sometime in the following weeks he ran into his neighbor again.

This time he asked her out for a coffee. She didn't seem to believe him when he said he just wanted to catch up but reluc-tantly agreed. No doubt she had met a 'Georgie' or two of her own.

This is when James revealed that the coffee date eventually turned into his life.

Waving his hands about James says with a dorky grin, "Julia I'd like to introduce you to my childhood neighbor who is now my wife, Josie." Donna and Julia both visibly surprised while Josie does a little twirl saying, "He's cute how he tells the story."

James said, "Over time we hung out more and got closer. Before you know it, we were a few years into our relationship when the question of marriage came up. She wasn't forcing me or anything. It was just the discussion of 'do you want to be married.' You know those conversations about how we see life going. Together and in general."

"It turns out everything I was ever looking for lived right nextdoor," James declared.

James continues his story, "I count myself as lucky to have remained close with childhood friends post marriage and kids. I realize that most people don't care for precisely the reasons I'm talking about.

"Leo and I had many discussions about how things changed after the initial incident with my mom. We had open and frank conversations about life. Mostly about how my mother said she wanted me to be as prepared as possible. Not only for life, in general but for the choices I would have to make.

"She'd say, 'if only I'd be this open with you growing up.' She explained that she wasn't afraid of telling me about her life and choices. However, she conceded that many parents are more afraid of admitting things about their lives that they let their children fall into the same tight spots.

"Of course, we spent many a conversation bashing old notions that children have to learn the hard way. It's about as idiotic an approach to parenting as I've heard at that point in my life.

"The very idea that a child must endure hardship and or pain to understand a concept I found downright lazy. Now that I'm a parent, I know that sometimes a child will simply not heed the advice or warnings given. As I see it, this is the child's choice, but to forgo the former 'because letting them do it is the only way they'll learn'--I don't even have the words.

James continues, "As I sit here telling you about the trail of hurt that led to my enlightenment. I regret so many choices. I worry about the pain I may have caused and realize that with a little bit more information, I might not have made the juvenile choices I did.

"The truth is that the whole thing infuriates me. I know it sounds selfish, but I can't help wondering what my life would have been like had I had this information sooner. Sure, I was young, and it might have taken several conversations and a multitude of learning moments, but I'm reminded of my children.

"I can't think of a time where I felt put out by giving them such important and life-altering information. Certainly not because I was simply too embarrassed."

Josie chimes in with her delightful humor. "I didn't spend years handling their poo for them to go making bad choices because you're too embarrassed to admit something that could help them make better ones."

To which Julia responds, "You can say that again." Prompted by a memory, Julia says, "Leo would say life is like one of those games he played. They were these virtual worlds where people from around the globe made characters and explored, adventured, and socialized. You could even group with all these people from anywhere in the world to defeat Boss level enemies. My Leo would say the thing about these characters is that they had to be leveled up. They could go from level 1 to, say, level 60. This means that as everyone plays the same content, your progress is often helped by online content that covers everything you are going to encounter and how to be victorious. Since he never met a player who didn't read up on things ahead of time or used guides to progress through specific content, it seemed curious that society seems to think our children should fend for themselves.

"Leo was adamant that our children view him the same as these resources. They were encouraged to ask him about anything whatsoever. He'd tell them that especially where the personal/private issues are uncomfortable to talk about, it would be much better to ask him and find out how he handled it than to make the same embarrassing mistakes he made. He'd remind them that 'it's easier to get past awkwardness with your dad than your friends. Think about it.'

She adds, "Sorry, just reminded me about Leo. He wasn't always successful, but the kids knew the door was open. He was just sometimes a little too challenging to talk to in general. Please continue."

James says, "No, it's okay. Fortuitous actually. I'm glad you remembered that because I got it from Leo, but I'll get to that.

First, let's fast forward to how I almost ruined our marriage before it started."

THIS ELICITS a surprised look from the ladies. Shifting their heads in Josie's direction, Julia and Donna are met with a smile while Josie places a box of tissues in front of each of them. Josie then points back to James.

Continuing, James says, "You see, it was just a few years ago I was laying in bed staring at the ceiling as the sun peeked over the horizon. I had been in that position most of the night with my mind on the day to come. I hadn't noticed the 8 minutes and 20 seconds worth of sunlight working its way across the room--that is until I got a face full of photons.

"After that, I quickly threw my hands up in front of my face, sat up, and took inventory. I thought to myself, 'This would be the best day so far in my life' and 'I would be loved forever.' It was a sensation I'd only felt once before--my mother, with her love and guidance, had finally, at this point in my life, convinced me that I should focus on being a better man and finding unconditional love.

"With my mother's help, I had found a path forward from a tumultuous upbringing navigating through a classic male egocentric youth to a place where I finally understood the falsehoods of my male role models. I realized more about love and its unconditional nature. Unsure I'd ever experienced it before, I had stopped looking for women who were hot and willing. I now know it was a standard as subjective as its application.

"Nonetheless, one which was attempted to transpose onto me subtly, all by the outdated male influence early in my life. It was everywhere you looked, and although my uncles and those males in my life considered me successful with the ladies, Mom and her experiences taught me just how wrong their approach was.

"Sure they thought me a ladies' man, but after a lot of reflection ..."

Donna interrupts James here. Looking at Julia, Donna says, "How did he do that?"

Julia replies with a smirk, "My man was a brain ninja."

James is curious and asks, "Um, what do you mean?"

Donna says, "We'll tell you about it later; please continue."

Meanwhile, Julia leans into Josie and whispers what she and Donna were talking about.

James begins to speak again, doing his best not to be distracted by all three of the ladies now giggling like school girls who passed a note.

"So there I was. My life had changed, and I knew in my heart that I had to stake the proverbial claim on the one I love. It was time that I proposed. I had made all the grand plans. I snuck around behind Josie's back for a few months coordinating things.

"I wanted the proposal to be the best thing she'd ever experienced. A bold claim I know, but I was ready. I had watched her favorite movies and paid close attention when she watched romantic movies. It would have been a scene right out of a film."

"Would have been?" Julia asks. A private smile is shared between Josie and James.

Josie leans down to Julia and loudly whispers, "Fade in Leo."

"Thank you, darling." James proclaims sarcastically. "Yes, this is where Leo enters the story.

"You see, that's how long it would take for me to feel I was ready to take things further with Josie. I was in a place where I thought I could give her a decent start in life. I had a long way to go to get where I wanted to be.

"This inevitably led to one of the most stressful days of my life. It was the day I decided to ask Josie to marry me."

Immediately, you could see the excitement it brings to Donna.

She is a self-admitted sucker for a good proposal story.

Julia jokes, "Donna is going for a record of proposals received."

Donna replies, "Let the man tell his story, or I'll ask you how many times you made Leo propose before putting him out of his misery."

Clearly, this was not a discussion Julia wanted to have. With a smile on her face and shooting Donna a look, she says, "Please, James continue."

James says, "So there I am …"

The ladies sit opposite James as he regales them with the anxiety and elation he felt. His story was finally going to change for good. Today at that.

James recounted how he was looking around the small studio apartment. Both so confident and yet terrified. He knew he had done everything he could possibly do to ensure the day's success and the happiness of his love. Still, he could not help contemplating the numerous things that could go wrong.

People being late, forgetting their assigned tasks or worse - other people unknowingly interrupting his plans. He has been planning this day for the last four months.

Since that day, he learned something about himself that he couldn't live without--he'd waited. He made a meaningful and consistent effort toward change. He felt certain that he was now on a new life path and a bit anxious to get it started.

As his mother would tell him every holiday, 'See how motivated you can be when you want something. Harness that, and you'll build an empire.'

James had arrived at a pivotal moment in his journey. His hopes were pinned to the idea that the world, at least his world, would see the new James he'd worked so hard on.

Hopefully, if all went well, his love would approve of the new him, and together their journey would begin.

"And then," James says, "the light bulb went on and I knew it was time."

. . .

Subtle gasps come from the ladies because everyone loves a good romantic story. Meanwhile James displayed a chuckle of embarrassment.

He admits he walked them into that because 'As Leo always said, if they are not interested in what you are saying, they are not likely to absorb or retain any of what you said.'

"If we weren't here for Leo, I'd … you're not making this up, are you?" Donna asks.

Quickly reassured by Josie that James is on the up and up, she injects, "Ladies, my husband is a college professor. He simply can't help but turn everything into a story he hopes you'll remember thoroughly. It's annoying as hell sometimes but makes him a wonderful professor. The students love his classes."

"You're off the hook, James, but I believe I owe you one. What happened next?" Julia asks.

"So there I was--the alarm sounding off--myself wondering for a moment if it was all a dream. Though, I was sitting up, it didn't truly hit me until I saw the tux hanging on the armoire. As quick as I could, I proceeded to get up and prepare. It was time and I remember thinking to myself how Leo would tell me that everything in life hinges on a single moment. For me it would be that moment I decided to chose my mom over a girl who I had no business....well, suffice to say that had it not been for the 15 minutes I left to drop her back at the party I wouldn't have needed that tux," James explains.

"Here is where things get visual," James continues. "Before we get to your specific questions, there is a video I'd like to show you. Leo recorded it for you and it might explain better than I can."

Grabbing the remote control from the coffee table, James turned to the ladies and asks, "Everyone ready? Drinks, snacks, tissues?"

Josie replies, "Check, check, and check."

James then hits play, and all eyes are on the television.

PEN PALS

As the video begins, you can see a backroom of a Denny's restaurant. Nothing seems out of the ordinary.

Then in the back corner of the screen … "That's my Leo!" Julia exclaims. "How? What? When?"

"Well, well, well," Donna adds.

Excitedly, Julia asks, "Donna, what is it?"

"Would you look at who is in the reflection?" Donna replies, continuing, "There. On the wall. Can you see her?"

They all scoured the screen with their eyes trying to figure out what Donna is talking about.

After a few seconds, Donna asks, "Don't you see anyone you recognize?"

Julia says, "Sure, that's Leo right there."

"Nobody else? Maybe younger and perhaps resembles you more than Leo?"

Julia then shouts excitedly, "What in the world is she doing there?"

One of the framed pictures, on the wall, offers a reflection of the person behind the camera. Donna explains to Josie that the young lady is Julia's granddaughter, Nova.

Josie explains that she and James knew. They just weren't sure if Nova would be noticed.

Donna and Julia exchange confused glances as James starts to explain that Nova helped Leo. "... well, it'd be best if you continue to watch before I get caught up in the details. Though, I should warn you, Julia, Nova is a bit anxious to find out how upset you are going to be with her. She loves Leo immensely, as you know.

"What you are going to learn is, in large part, due to her efforts to help Leo. She helped with the 'contribute' portion of his mantra--Consider, Create, & Contribute. I'm sure you've heard it before."

Julia smirks. "Maybe once or twice."

"She took excellent care of him, so you shouldn't be upset," James says.

Julia chimes in with, "Don't give it another thought. I understand why she would be concerned. They had a unique relationship. In some ways, she seemed to idolize Leo, almost as a big brother. It's the closest description of what they had.

"For them, the generational divide was but a blip in their conversations. They just got along so well, like pals. It's largely why I would never worry for one second where she and Leo are concerned. The worse he got, the more she cared for him like he was her own. Strange way to describe it, perhaps, but I suppose it's one of those things that lacks a single description. If she took him somewhere or helped him with something, I'm confident she had a reason and always looked out for his best interest. Now, as for why she kept it from me, I have a good feeling Leo was behind it all."

"There's my guy," Josie says, getting everyone's attention back on the screen.

On the screen, there is a slightly younger James sitting next to Leo.

Then Leo speaks,

"Hi, Babe!"

He waves to the screen--presumably waving at Julia.

Julia breathes in. It is like he is right there talking to her. She is not mentally prepared for this.

JAMES QUICKLY HITS the pause button, and the ladies check to make sure Julia is okay.

She takes a few deep breaths before answering, "I'm fine. Let it continue."

James hits the play button, and Leo continues talking,

"Well, I guess you've found James. I never doubted it. Much like I don't doubt that you are a little perturbed with me."

Leo stares into the camera and smiles before blowing a kiss.

"I love you, Noodle. I hope I didn't disturb your life too much. I'm sure you were very busy sitting at home."

His sarcasm brings a glow to Julia.

"The reason you are watching this is because I wanted to introduce you to my friend, James,"

"I'm sure you know a little at this point, but James will explain the rest. He's a good kid. He will take care of the big chest until you are ready for it. If you only want it a little at a time, he can help. Just talk to him--it is all real."

Leo suddenly changes topics,

"Buttercup, honey, say hi to your grandma."

Turning the camera around, Nova looks into the camera.

"Hi Grandma, I hope you aren't too upset with me. I'm taking good care of him. Pop is following my rules, and I'm screening everyone. Love you."

Julia says, "See, I told you I didn't have to worry about Leo when he was with Nova."

JAMES PAUSES the video and says, "I know it's not much, but I promised I'd show it. He also left you a personal video. I'll send it when you leave so you can watch it privately at home.

"He was my friend. We may not have been best friends, yet somehow the impact he's had on my life was transformative. Just ask my wife.

"His sage wisdom provided a calm and sound perspective when the situation made it difficult for most to see past emotions. Talking to him and hearing his take on things … I was surprised by the strange things he'd say at the most unusual times. More often than not at wholly inappropriate times. Still, having him in my life has only served to elevate it.

"As I look back, the source of these events were all rooted in the heart of a man child with no verbal filter. He certainly didn't resemble a child, but if you spent enough time with him, you'd understand.

"Whether it was pointing out the obvious with the delicacy of a child or reverting to his child-like need for his Noodle's attention, comfort, and love, the transformation was heartbreaking.

"In a split second, inspiration could strike, and he would turn to the deep philosophical contemplation of a seasoned academic. The change was seamless, and without warning. I can't tell you how many times … well, you know.

"I'm sure we can all readily admit it was absolutely infuriating at times. Being his friend comes with tests of one's inner strength.

At times, conversations with him seemed almost implausible. It's not that he didn't use words or understand words. He could be quite eloquent. The real trouble was only apparent to those with the patience and sight to have noticed that he was more than what he appeared.

"Utterly heartbreaking to see a man blessed with a rare mind cut off from that brain and shifted into a man who contentedly existed on snacks, youthful diversions, and his Noodle."

Julia smiles with tears in her eyes at hearing James use her pet name. Having lived through it, she knows what James is talking about but to hear it come out of a stranger's mouth …. In this moment, it felt nice to hear she'd made such an impression on her Leo. She is pleased knowing Leo had found it worth using to help also make one on James' life.

James continues, "I later learned these were misleading notions of his existence. As you know, he loved telling people, 'I'm living a Buddhist dream.'

"I believe if it weren't for you, Julia, he might have given up long ago. You were the focal point of his existence. The way he put it. 'She is what makes getting out of bed every morning worthwhile.'

"You know when I first met Leo, it was at a wedding. I had been running late. When I arrived, I found my lady love engaged in a conversation with you and some gentlemen." James continues, "After months of planning, it was meant to be a wedding proposal she couldn't refuse. Yet, I didn't even end up asking her. I can say it is here that Leo enters."

James explains he'd spoken to his Josie ahead of time, apologizing that he'd be a little late. As always, she was understanding and just told him to look for her near the tables. She had been excited all week because she was going to see an old coworker, Julia, whom James had heard about often.

"Now when I saw the way the man seemed to cater to Josie, it caught my attention. Laughing and agreeing. I'm not sure I've ever seen anyone nod in agreement that much in one conversation. There was admittedly jealousy at play, but can you blame me? I was already late, and now some guy was showering her with his attention. I saw nothing good coming from it.

"Hey there, beautiful," I say as I see Josie approach.

I guess I had strewn over the jerk at the table too and didn't notice her.

She says, "Hi, hon, we are just having a work-related conversation, and I didn't want you to walk right into it." *Oh.* Then she says, "Just grab a seat over there, and I'll be done in a sec. So glad you are here."

I tell her that "I'd wait an eternity for you, sweetness." She smiles, and before she can give me a kiss and head back, I ruin it. I don't know why I say it, but I blurt out, "Make sure he knows you are mine."

With a stupid smile, some part of my brain thought this was a romantic way to stake one's claim out of love and man's inherent right. You know the residuals of what my role models taught me.

As I brace for the consequences, I know it is bad. I'm not sure how or why, but I know. The real question going through my mind at the moment is, 'why is it so quiet?'

I realize her only reaction is to kiss my cheek and say, "Grab a seat." With a brief pause, she makes a shaky fist. With what can only be called an angry smile says, "You can be such a stupid head. I'll be right back."

All I can do in that moment is stare at her as she returns to her conversation. The guy is all smiles and a tad too touchy-feely for my tastes.

Then I hear a voice, "What if I told you he was secretly gay?"

Thinking out loud, I say, "That would probably make me feel better."

I turn around toward the voice and find the owner. There is a guy sitting in a chair with a cane. He looked older--well older than me at least--I'd say he was in his forties.

A bit embarrassed by my reply, I say, "Sorry, I thought you were talking to me."

To which he replies, "No, it's fine. I was talking to you. I'm guessing that's the young lady motivating you?"

I'm sitting in the seat next to him. He keeps talking, "I hope you don't mind me saying, but you aren't doing yourself any favors."

"Is he really gay?" I ask him.

"If you must know," he replies, "I have no idea. What you should be asking yourself is what difference does it make?"

So I tell him.

"Duh, a gay guy being friendly isn't the threat that a straight guy flirting is."

"Oh, I get it," he says. "If he is straight, then he has a chance at your girl, but if he likes men, then she has nothing he wants. Well, I guess that would make sense to you. Thanks for explaining it."

I look at the guy and say, "Sounds like that doesn't make much sense to you. Is this a problem for you?"

"No problem at all, really. I just can't help but wonder what you really know about what's going on over there," he says.

"Who is this guy? I think to myself," explains James, "but don't want to be rude. I decide to play along."

I tell him, "Okay, I'll bite. My girlfriend is talking to an old friend and some guy I don't know. I've never seen him before. I guess the man in me doesn't like it. To be honest, he seems too hands-on."

"Wow," I continue, "I bet that sounded shallow. I apologize if I'm a bit short; I'm usually not so high-strung. I just had a big day planned today, and I'm a little nervous, I suppose."

"Like 'The Big Day?'" He asks.

"Yes, that big day. Don't say anything. It's not time yet." I check my texts to ensure everyone is in place.

"Well, congrats--what is your name again?" he asks.

"Apologies. My name is James. It's been a day as you might imagine," I reply.

He replies, "No, it's quite alright. I remember all the nerves a proposal can bring on. At your age, I'm guessing you've already gone through any doubts you might have had."

I say, "Yeah, I've been through all that in my head. I knew without a doubt that I want to spend my life with her. My nerves are more a result of execution than worry." Then, I proceed to tell him my plan.

He seems to be thinking through what I am saying. He repeats some of it back to himself while doing this thing with his fingers. It is like his finger is chalk, and he is working out the math in the air in front of him.

I just continue to tell him my plan while watching him work it out on his magic 'board.' All the while, I am wondering if his result will somehow calm my nerves.

Now for some reason, he says, "Do you know who is getting married today?"

Well, of course, I do. It is a current coworker of my wife. I tell him so, and he replies, "Oh, I didn't realize they were so close."

"I didn't say they were close. I said they worked together. I don't think they hang out much, if at all outside of work. You know I'm not sure how well they know each other."

He says, "My apologies. I figured they were close. I mean the way you had arranged to attach your wedding proposal with the bride's wedding day. Now, my wife, she would never be able to enjoy an important life event in those kinds of circumstances unless it was intentional.

"Your lady must be exceedingly patient and understanding with you. That's cool. I've always said some people are just big balls of sweet in spite of their thoughtless mates. You are lucky…"

And I interrupt him.

"Wait. What?" I ask, hoping for a better explanation.

He says, "Well look, we are at a wedding, so if you propose and get engaged here, it will always be tied to your marriage. I don't mean there is anything wrong with it, but my experience tells me that ladies might not be okay with that. Some might even suggest it is a sign of thoughtlessness. In any case, I trust you know your dearest better than I. Please excuse my mouth-- it makes it hard to keep friends as you might imagine, so I just run at the mouth when I get a chance to talk to folks. I mean no harm."

SUDDENLY, things get quiet. We just sit there. It is an awkward silence, I suppose. In truth, Leo's words feel as though they are slowly beginning to haunt me. In the back of my head, his words are cycling and repeating themselves. The processing of his words feel more significant somehow. It troubles me as I sit watching the love of my life carry on her conversation. The troll left, and she is laughing with her friend.

As I sit, watching her, I am overcome with a memory of her.

She talked about work and how this guy at work was kissing her ass lately because she had a report to finish that would somehow decide his future. Now I don't think she was his supervisor. If my memory was to be believed, she actually told me about him.

He had lied about something at work, and a report she was working on would prove it. He knew--she knew it, and no one had asked for it yet, but its natural cycle makes it due next week. She'd already told him no one owned her, and she would give it to management if asked; otherwise, she'd produce the report when it was due as usual.

His groveling and kissing up was pointless. I knew my--right not my--but rather, I knew she would not be taken in by such dishonesty. She would do her job honorably. 'It's who she is.'

I turn to Leo and say, "I hope you don't mind me saying, but you are one odd duck."

Of course, he doesn't mind, and then mumbles, 'odd duck' to himself a few times before stopping.

I tell him he helped clear something up for me and relieved the anxiety I'd been feeling for days. I show him my phone while in the middle of contacting all the friends who helped me set up this proposal.

Holding up the screen, he can see the sent text message that reads, 'Hi gang. Thank you for all of your assistance and preparation. Unfortunately, I have to call an abort on the plan. No, we are absolutely okay. Better than ever. Really. I'll just say the mission is aborted. Another project is in motion. Be in touch tomorrow.'

"Wordy but clear," he says. "Why the change of heart?"

Oh, this guy! I say, "You know why. I don't know why or how, but you knew what you were doing."

JAMES COMES out of his memory and explains to the girls that this is when he realized this whole time he was talking to Julia's 'needy' broken husband.

Julia looks perplexed at the memory James just shared. She is only now remembering that she had met James. The wedding happened so long ago.

James continues to tell them that he had gotten some of the best advice one could hope for on that day. He's glad Leo pointed out how botched the proposal was. He didn't even feel stupid realizing any of this. The advice was sound, and Leo made him feel like it was all his idea. The help Leo had provided had an air of accidental, but James knew in his heart that Leo's advice was in some way intentional.

"Before he left the wedding," James tells them. "Leo handed me a business card and said, 'I'd love to hear more about your realizations and choices.' I sat there, staring at his card. A simple card. A symbol I didn't recognize on one side and a PO box on the other side. No cell phone. No email. Just the symbol and PO box.

"Now you may not be surprised to find out that Josie and I got engaged a few weeks later in spectacular fashion--for us. I can confirm it was a surprise to her even after telling her the events of the previous attempt.

"After our engagement, Josie told me more about Leo and the

PO box, explaining how writing made it easier to communicate with friends because of his brain damage. It was easier for him to understand reading it slowly, maybe sometimes more than once before replying. The writing also makes his replies easier for him to communicate in return.

"Josie told me that she'd talked to Julia about it before and explained it all to me. His troubles and his structured way of doing things and why. I understand how it might drive people away, so I decided then I would reply. That is how we became pen pals."

DOIT

J ames looks at Julia and says, "I hope that explains some things. As for what we are up to, it's quite simple. We were penpals. I assume Nova helped him after a while. Leo had several pen pals, but Nova kept the list small.

"Before you worry, let me assure you they were all positive connections--marriages, partnerships, friendships, and even a small business. I believe I can say with a level of certainty I don't think anyone can say Leo specifically said he wanted it like this. Still, his occasional smirk and comment suggested he liked how it unfolded over time."

Julia asks James, "What about 'The Order'?"

"Oh, right, I almost forgot. That is a guild for an online game most of us play. Some would say that since Leo spent so much time there, it was easiest to reach him online when we had a question. You know he was good with the odd info on things. Some of us were already players, and others started after meeting Leo. As Leo would say, it simply evolved to meet our needs."

James smiles a little bit, and right away, Julia puts her hand on his arm and says, "I'm so sorry. You must miss him too."

She watches as James wipes a tear from the corner of his eye and replies, "I was asked to deliver a message from a group of folks like myself. Friends of Leo. People who'd shared similar experiences with him. Simply put, we are all very thankful for the influence he had on our lives. We will all miss him but hope he's found his peace beyond the rim. More importantly, we want to thank you. Leo was fond of saying the only reason he hadn't given up was your love. Despite his challenges, you never intentionally made him feel like the broken man he knew he was. It was a testament to your capacity to love him.

"Without what you gave him, he would never have accidentally-on-purpose been able to help us in our lives. For that alone, we owe you just as much as him. If you need anything, you just ask. Please take this card and never hesitate. Consider us all your children in some non-weirdo way."

James continues, "If you need a tree trimmed, lawn mowed, anything. Text one thing or ten things you need around the house. Life is unkind, and Leo's one wish was you never having to worry about the little things--for the rest of your days. We vowed we would do just that. Before you object, understand that it will always just be a person who would do no less for his/her mother. So please never doubt the sincerity."

Julia sits for a moment and absorbs this new information about her Leo. This entire day has been a lot to process.

She feels she should be upset about this secret life her husband had going on to some degree. She also wonders what, if anything, she should do regarding Nova.

Donna is the ultimate best friend and notices the mental drain that is beginning to take effect on Julia. "Well, folks, it has truly been an adventure," Donna exclaims.

Right on cue, Julia recognizes she's reached her mental capacity for the day, if not surpassed it.

"However," Donna continues, "I think it's time to get this little lady back home. I'm under strict instructions, as you know."

The relief on Julia's face is visible. She did her best to be friendly and polite but everything is starting to weigh her down. She hasn't had a moment alone to decompress, and she can't wait to get back home to repeatedly watch the video Leo left for her.

If there is one thing she's been wanting for weeks now, it is to see Leo once more--and it is waiting for her at home.

Julia says, "I can't thank you all enough--new friends and old. It will be days before I can process all this new information. Were it not for Leo and his Love Magic, I would probably still be sitting at our kitchen table."

"You should all take note of this," Julia continues, "This random kind of craziness is what Leo was always bringing to our lives. Not the bad kind, just this emotional, reflective kind. In his heart, he wanted everyone to love and be loved. Leo wanted people to appreciate themselves and those around them. He truly wanted everyone to see the beauty in themselves even if he couldn't see his own.

"His heart ached at the suffering of others, especially when it felt obvious to him how to change things. I'm glad to have learned something about Leo's life that I didn't know. Pen pals were something that brought joy and love to his life. Thank you all for your part in that."

Hugs are shared, and once James reminds her to let him know when she is ready to start the chest of letters, Julia and Donna leave.

GETTING IN THE CAR, Donna says, "Well, I bet that it's not how you expected that to go. I know I didn't. It was nice, though, right? Once again, I am jealous of you." Then Donna makes a declaration Julia doesn't expect. "Tomorrow, I am reaching out to David. There will be no prior discussion. We will see what he says, and I'll get back to you."

"Good for you. Are we there yet?" Julia asks with a smirk.

Taking less time to get back to Julia's than it does to get to James, the ride is tranquil despite Julia's impatience.

"Would you mind if I stopped off at Wally World. I need to grab a few things for your kitchen," Donna asks.

Julia says, "My darling friend, you have two choices. You can drive me home and accept whatever supplies I currently have or you can drop me off at home and then go to the store. Either way, there is a video of my beloved waiting for me. The only remaining option is for me to take your car and leave you to do whatever you feel. Does that work for you?"

Donna laughs. "I was going to say that I'm going to stay the night should you need me. I get it, but geez, maybe I should get a padlock for the door to my murderous friend."

Seconds later, they both burst into laughter, soon to be followed by a few random tears.

Arriving at Julia's, she scurries inside and grabs her laptop. Donna sees to the drinks and brings wine over to the living room.

They make themselves comfortable on the couch. Julia fires up the laptop and opens her email. Sure enough, James had sent it while they were there.

Before she hits play, Donna grabs her hand and says, "Wait, do you have enough tissues? Need anything else?"

"Why does my best friend insist on bringing out my ugly? Can I press play, or should I get to snapping boney fingers?" Smiling her less effective attempt at an intimidating face, Donna gets the hint--not funny.

Hitting play, they both sit back and watch.

The intro is slow, like he turned it on and forgot about it for a second. Movement begins with Leo entering the room and sitting on his bed. There he is in his Mountain apartment. Leo in the flesh--sort of.

Julia is quiet and stoic. Her attention is focused on the moment Leo enters the screen.

He begins talking,

"Hi, babe. I hope this finds you well. There are a great many things I wanted to discuss with you that I couldn't say in front of the others. A list of all those answers you might be needing questions to."

She is studying every inch of his face, how he talked, his words, even his mannerism. The kind of studying one does when they don't want to forget. It is like she is preparing for the ultimate "all about Leo" exam and doesn't want to miss an iota of information.

Julia knows she can watch and rewatch. She also knows she will.

He continues,

"What to do with this and that, where to put things, you know. I'm sorry, what? That's not what you want to talk about. Well, sugar, what do you want to talk about? What are you wearing?"

Julia interrupts with, "Oh My Lord."

Donna goes to pause it, and Julia says, "Let it play. He's trying to make me smile like a dork that he is. He wouldn't embarrass me, and if his Love Magic is worth a damn then he would know you are sitting here."

Nervous but committed, Julia watches on. Back on the screen, "No, Donna, you can't change it. Don't hate on our passionate love."

The women exchange a glance as Leo cracks up laughing.

Leo continues,

"Now before you start making fun of me, especially you, Donna, I want to remind you that I'm trying to make this video while talking to no one and anticipating your future reactions. How do you like me now, Donna? I know she's there. Hi, Donna, thanks for all the help you've given Julia; she's your best friend but still. Thank you for being there when I can't."

Leo then moves on to a list of items and topics that are of no interest to Donna. While it all has practical meaning for Julia, she wanted to hear his voice go on the way he used to. She would get back to the information itself later. The video lasts for about an hour.

In the video, Leo explains he made a compilation of videos that would be sent to Julia over the week to avoid emotional overload. Today's compilation is long and random so Julia can use it to feel like he is there, especially when she needs help falling asleep. For that, he'd made a few of him reading books to Julia.

The videos will cover the gamut--birthday songs, love songs, keeping her company in the tub, helping her get to sleep, and even just sitting at his desk playing games. A video for all occasions he could think of.

HER SOUL WOULD REST EASIER NOW KNOWING Leo had all these good memories with him.

Somehow, she is relieved. Relieved that Leo had found a way to interact with the world around him. It brings soft tears to her eyes to know Leo had finally found some kind of place in the world. Anyone who's spent enough time at home understands the impact of having a place in the outside world on one's life.

For many years, Julia struggled both literally and figuratively with his inability to find a place. She found herself making excuses for others so he wouldn't feel bad.

He knew it might seem overboard to most, but it was who he was. Why should Julia have to go without only to make others comfortable?

"Preposterous," he'd say.

He had vowed when he found out he was sick to take every possible step to alleviate her suffering, and this was part of that plan. Listening is up to her, but he decided she should have the option.

FOR THE NEXT FEW HOURS, they drink wine while Julia flips through the videos he had sent. Among them is one called,

"DOIT."

For the life of her, Julia can't recall that word. She suspects it's an acronym. Donna suggests it's a video game reference. Julia hits play.

The screen darkens. As the lens of the video camera focuses, Julia immediately hits stop, and both ladies laugh out loud, "Oooooooh!! Do It."

Donna giggles. "I guess you do keep secrets. I never realized he was so … athletic?"

Julia shyly replies, "You shut your mouth. It was our one video from a memory that I am most definitely not sharing with you until I'm on my deathbed." Julia smiles with red in her cheeks.

Suddenly, Julia stretches out her arms and yawns. "Boy, am I tired," Julia says. "I think I'm going to turn in and get some rest. It's been a long day."

"You are a lying slut, but you deserve it." With a smile, Donna gets up as they prepare to head off to their rooms for the night.

Before exiting the living room, Donna says, "Hey Julia, mind if I borrow that video when you're finished with it?"

A few seconds later, Donna drops her stuff as Julia nails her with a couch cushion and replies, "Good night, hater! Be ready in the morning. I'm calling James first thing to bring over the writing chest."

With a smile on her face that she's not known since before Leo moved on, Julia rushes off.

For the first time in what seems like an eternity, Julia feels as though she is preparing to reconnect with her love, maybe even learn to say goodbye. She has the strangest feeling that she might even be able to live once again.

> "Make the most of each moment,
> until we meet again on this side of the Rim "
> ~ Leonard Sebastian Runkel